Feeling the eyes of the Seven on him, Simon stepped to the near center of the room, attracting even more of the demons' attention.

"For those of you who do not know of me, I call myself Simon Tombs. I am Lord Mage of Fairie and the tamer of demons. I have sent many of your kind back to the Pit and I have dared Hell itself in order to rescue repentant souls. I do not fear you because, just as you might know me, I know you. I know you all. I have read the Book, the first book that was carved soon after the Fall of Man. It contains the names of all those cast out of Paradise. I've read and memorized the names and can pronounce them in the First Language. Do any of you dare challenge me?"

Simon paused to judge the effect. The djinn had stopped swirling, the lesser demons withdrew into their containers. On the walls, six of the Deadly Sins now seemed to be avoiding his gaze, with only Pride daring to look at him.

PADWOLF PUBLISHING BOOKS BY JOHN L. FRENCH

Here There Be Monsters, a Bianca Jones collection
Monsters Among Us, a Bianca Jones collection
The Last Monster, a Bianca Jones collection
The Devil of Harbor City
Past Sins
Rites Of Passage: a DMA casefile of Agent Karver and Bianca Jones (with Patrick Thomas)
The Grey Monk: Souls on Fire
The Nightmare Strikes
Bad Cop, No Donut (editor)
Mermaids 13 (editor)
Camelot 13 (editor with Patrick Thomas)
Frankenstein:Monsters of the Abyss (with Patrick Thomas)
Murder At Castle Dracula (with Patrick Thomas)
Staring Into The Abys (editor with Patrick Thomas)
The Abyss Stares Back (editor with Patrick Thomas)
Bullets & Brimstone: a Mystic Investigators™ book (with Patrick Thomas) featuring Bianca Jones
From The Shadows: a Mystic Investigators™ book (with Patrick Thomas) featuring the Nightmare

OTHER BOOKS BY JOHN L. FRENCH

The Last Redhead
Paradise Denied
Blood is the Life, a Bianca Jones collection
The Wages of Syn
When the Devil Drives
Death on Omega Station
The Assassins' Ball (with Patrick Thomas)
To Hell in a Fast Car (editor)
With Great Power (editor with Greg Schauer)

Simon Tombs: The Wine of Cana

John L. French

PADWOLF
PUBLISHING

PADWOLF PUBLISHING INC.
WWW.PADWOLF.COM
www.facebook.com/Padwolf

SIMION TOMBS: The Wine Of Cana
© 2025 John L. French

cover art and design by Patrick Thomas

ISBN 13 digit 978-1-958310-13-7
Printed in the USA First Printing

On October 28, 2023, many of us gathered to say goodbye to the Delta Marriot Hotel in Hunt Valley, home to more conventions than I can remember. Some of us sat in the lobby, loudly discussing how we might steal the silver horses on one of the walls. (Not that we would, we're writers, planning impossible things is what we do.) Afterwards, we went to the Green Turtle for lunch. The next day, one of our group sent a message to Green Turtle complimenting the food and the service. In doing so, he gave us all nicknames. Because of my former profession (CSI) and the city in which I worked and lived (Baltimore), I was dubbed "Detective Charm."

Fast forward to November 22. I was writing the story "Playing with Fire" for this collection and needed a name for a detective. Remembering the name I was given, I called him Detective Charm. He was supposed to be a walk-on — show up, take Simon Tombs to where he had to be, and exit, stage right. Instead, he insisted on hanging around. I learned that he was a reformed dodgy cop who had married an angel and he wound up playing a major part in several stories.

So, for dubbing me "Detective Charm" and thereby inspiring an integral character in this book, *Simon Tombs: The Wine of Cana* is dedicated to:

Jay Smith

Contents

The Bridge

There is a great chasm between Paradise and Perdition, and no one can cross from one to the other. So said the Redeemer, quoting Abraham.

But even Eternity changes, albeit ever so slowly. First, there was a tiny thread of hope, hope that the ever-lasting punishments of Hell might not be so eternal. Some, it was said, had escaped its tortures.

As this belief spread, the tiny thread grew. It became a cord, and the cord became a rope, and the rope a bridge. And from that bridge there came a light, one that shone in the darkness of Hell, calling those whose souls shone as brightly as it did. These were the Repentant of Hell, who had come to regret their sins and the suffering they had caused, and who finally earned forgiveness, not only from the Divine but also from themselves.

Only these could cross the Bridge.

But the Lords of Perdition did not willingly allow them to cross. Their progress was contested every step of the way. Those who despaired did not reach it. Only those with Hope and Faith succeeded.

But Hell still does not easily give up its damned. Those demons closest to the Bridge would seize the repentant ones and throw them into the chasm to begin their journey anew.

Until the Guardian came.

Joy to the World

It was the custom of Sebastian's to stay open continuously beginning at nine p.m. on December 23rd through St. Stephan's Day, and again from sunset on New Year's Eve until the second day of the new year. The holidays were a time for friends and family and there were those who had neither. Sebastian's stayed open to give these people a place to not be alone.

While Simon Tombs had no immediate family, he did have many friends, any one of whom would have been glad to have played host to him. But Simon was not in a sociable mood that season. He had recently lost someone dear to him and, although he believed that she had moved on to better things, he still missed her. He was used to missing and losing friends and lovers, such is the curse of a very long life, but Fel had been very special to him. In addition, Simon had not heard from or seen Caitlin Hood since the detective sergeant had learned the true nature of Good and Evil in a downtown parking garage.

So Simon sat in Sebastian's and drank whatever concoction Murphy made up — this year the house special was a "Twisted Elf" — and ate food provided by the Lombard Street Sandwich Shop, Mead's BBQ, and Patterson's Pizzas.

The music had just switched over from traditional Christmas songs to instrumental Celtic when she walked in. There was a radiance about her, a certain gleam in her eye, and her feet did not quite touch the floor.

She walked, or rather glided over to him. "For you, Simon Tombs," she said in a voice like a song. She handed him an envelope.

"Fan mail from some flounder?"

"No," she replied, "this is what I really call a message."

With that, she was gone as if she had never been there. Judging by the lack of reaction from the others present, perhaps she had not.

Staring at the envelope, Simon dared hope. He opened it slowly — good news should be savored, bad news delayed. The note inside read only, "Tonight. The Empire State Building, 2 a.m." It was not signed nor was it in Fel's hand.

Simon looked at his watch. It was Christmas Eve, just past midnight. Two hours to get from Baltimore to New York. Plenty of time for him. In fact, he had time for another drink and maybe another slice.

An hour later, Simon arrived at Baltimore's Pennsylvania Station by cab. Other than a minimal staff, there was no one else there. He took one look around the century-old building then sat on one of the long wooden benches and prepared himself for his trip north.

The Universe has its rules. There are things that it allows and things that it will not permit. People like Simon Tombs knew their way around these rules. They knew the loopholes and the exceptions and the ways to twist and trick the Universe into doing what they and not it wanted.

Baltimore had a Pennsylvania Station. New York City had a Pennsylvania Station. Both served the same function, to convey passengers by rail from one place to another. These similarities were enough for Simon. He closed his eyes in one and imagined the other, a place much larger and much, much busier. One that was almost as crowded at two in the morning as it was at two in the afternoon. In his mind, Simon imagined the two Penn Stations as paired, miss-matched quantum particles linked together however much they were separated by distance. Then with his eyes still closed, he took the envelope from his coat pocket. The note inside was his orders, his mission, his ticket as it were. Then he dared the Universe to deny the sender of the note. After a moment, Simon felt the Universe relent. He said a quiet thanks and stood. Knowing that one day there would be a price to pay, there always is, Simon Tombs walked out of Baltimore's Pennsylvania Station and found himself on 7th Avenue and West 34th Street in New York City.

The streets of Gotham were, as always, busy. People on business, tourists on holiday, predators looking for targets, lonely people looking for friendship or love, lovers looking only at each other. Simon stopped for a moment to savor the atmosphere, aware of how many possible adventures there were just at that intersection. But he had an appointment 86 floors above 34th Street and it would not be polite to keep whoever it might be waiting.

The Empire State Building was closed for the night. It would not open to the public for hours, when it would admit people who had paid to watch the sunrise from the top of one of the most iconic buildings in the world.

The front doors were, of course, locked. But Simon had a way with doors and locks. A small glamour keeping him from being noticed by anyone inside or outside the building, he walked up to one door and whispered, "You, door, are all doors. All doors are you. I know you and now you know me. Please open as is your function and nature." A simple pull and Simon was inside.

The elevators were just as cooperative and soon Simon was standing alone on the open observation deck of the 86th floor. It seemed smaller than the first time he had visited and it was now surrounded by black iron fencing, which was high and curved to prevent despairing people from taking the quick way to the street.

Simon looked at his watch. It was just a few minutes short of 2 a.m. Given the nature of his summons, he did not expect anyone to come from inside the building. Instead, he walked the deck and watched the sky.

Several sets of church bells tolled out two o'clock on Christmas Eve when one of the stars separated itself from its fellows and began its descent. For a moment, it was the brightest object in the sky, then dimmed as it approached. When it got close, it was still bright enough for Simon to make out its form — human-shaped with wings that were as wide as it, or rather, she was tall.

When the angel flew over the barriers and alighted before Simon, he saw that she was dark-skinned with long, black hair. The feathers of her wings were ash-grey except for the ones on the tips. These were blackened as if burnt in a fire.

She was not the angel for whom Simon had hoped, but still, she was an angel, one of power and majesty, and Simon had to resist the urge to kneel in front of her. Instead, he bowed deeply. "Simon Tombs at your service."

Folding her wings, the angel returned the bow. "I am Nika, and your help is needed, Simon Tombs."

"What do you need of me?"

"Claus is missing, and you must find him."

Just then there was a machine sound. "The elevator," Simon said. "They're coming to get ready for the sunrise visitors."

"Then we must go down."

Simon looked over the edge. "Are you suggesting …"

Nika shrugged. "It's either that or walk 86 floors."

It was, Simon later remarked, a unique experience, descending to the streets of New York in the arms of an angel. They embraced each other tightly, she spread her wings, and together they left the observation deck. She did not, however, merely lower him to 34th Street. Instead, she flew up, then north toward Central Park.

"Where are we going?" Simon asked.

"Flying," came her reply. "I love to fly. Despite the wings, I don't do it enough. Only when I come to Earth."

As she swooped over the trees, only the children looked up. "I love this city," she said. "So many people, both good and bad. It is so full of life. I can understand why Claus chose to remain here."

Simon, too, was enjoying the flight. He was also enjoying being held tight against Nika's very feminine body and decided if what he was thinking and feeling was any sort of sin, he'd gladly do penance for it.

"Nika, about Claus?"

"Not up here, wait until we land."

Nika alighted in front of St. Patrick's Cathedral. She smiled. Her wings unfurled to their fullest and she let out what could only have been a sigh of joy.

"Feel it, Simon. Feel the Presence. The Divine are everywhere but here, here it is special. When this is over, we must visit."

She led him to Rockefeller Plaza where they found a place to sit in front of Prometheus and the ice rink. It was still early morning and too soon for skaters.

"Before we start talking about Claus, Nika, perhaps you should hide your wings."

"Why? This is New York. People are used to seeing impossible things before breakfast."

Simon had to agree. "So, tell me about Claus. Why is he missing and why can't They find him? If They have numbered the hairs on my head and know how many grains of sand there are on the beach, why can't They find this Claus? And are we talking Claus as in Santa Claus, the Spirit of Christmas, the giver of gifts, eight reindeer, and all that?"

"He doesn't have reindeer. He likes to travel by bus."

"Is he one of your kind?"

"He was part of the Host but … Claus did not fall, not exactly. Let us say he stumbled. It is easy to love humanity. The Divine do and we do as well. But Claus, he loved a little too much. He refused to return when summoned, choosing instead to stay among you. For most of the year that means helping in secret. This time of year, however … He is the Spirit of Christmas, so much so that he took the name of one of its symbols. It is his love that makes this a special time. People feel it and most are kinder, more generous, and more loving. But now I do not feel him."

"Maybe he's not in New York."

"This time of the year, he's always in New York. From the end of the Macy's parade until the ball drops, Claus is here. And it is from here that his joy of the season spreads across the country."

Simon had a thought. "They don't know you're here, do They?"

"They know, and They care, but ... I am here on my own. I, too, have a special love for Humanity. I have fought for it; I have burned for it." Nika moved her wings to display their burned feathers. "Claus and I are friends. He is missing and I must find him. We must find him. He serves humankind so it is only right that one of you helps find him."

"Not that I won't help, but why me?"

"When one of the Fallen seeks Redemption, it is noticed. And so is the one who led her to seek it."

"How is Fel?"

"She is closer to Paradise, but she is not yet there. But she has a purpose and is content."

"For that alone, I will help you."

"Thank you, Simon. How do we start?"

That is the question, Simon thought. *How do I find one being in a city of millions? Let's try it the easy way and see if that works.*

"Nika, may I touch you?"

"Our embrace as we flew from the tower was not enough?" she asked with a certain smile, a smile he had seen on the faces of many women, a smile that hinted and suggested, but in no way promised. It was a smile for later.

"Our embrace was almost too much, Nika, and yet not enough. But now I ask to touch you more closely, not your body but your self, your essence. Knowing that, I can search for Claus's."

Nika hesitated. "What you ask, Simon, is akin to touching the Divine. We were the first of Creation and much of the Creator is within us. You may not survive."

"I have risked that much for lesser causes. For the Spirit of Christmas, for you, I would risk all." Simon returned the angel's smile with one of his own, one that told her that there was nothing he would not dare, not if adventure was offered and the cause was right.

"Yes, I believe you would. But you're no use to me if you're a pile of ashes." Nika thought for a moment, then a sword of fire appeared in her hand, the heat it gave off warming the chilly morning.

The sword shrank down to a dagger. Running her thumb along its edge, she drew blood. "Will this do?"

"We shall see." Simon touched her thumb, transferring the angel blood to his finger. He closed his eyes and began his search.

Sensing what he was doing — it was, after all, her blood — Nika said, "If you need a map, we could fly over the city again."

A whispered, "No." Simon did not need a map. In another time, under another name, he had briefly made New York his home. While there he had tried to avoid trouble but, as always, it had found him. So did the police, one detective in particular, who suspected him of many things, only some of which he had done.

With Rockefeller Plaza as his starting point and the angel blood burning its way under his skin and into his soul, his mind spread out, seeking to match like with like. Manhattan first, then one by one the other boroughs. He spread his search into New Jersey.

He found nothing. *Why should it be easy?* Simon thought. *Except for twins, no two humans have the same DNA. Why should angels be any different?* That led him to wonder why angels, being spirits, would have blood at all, or need DNA.

As if reading his thoughts, Nika said, "When we come to Earth, we assume human form. We can be hurt; we can be killed. Which is why I fear for Claus. He sees the good in everyone, even when there is little of it there."

"What happens if you die?"

"Our spirit returns to the Essence from whom we are reborn. But Claus has been in mortal form for centuries. He may have bonded to it. So who can say what may happen?"

The Plaza skating rink was beginning to fill, a sign that the day was truly starting, a warning that time was passing. Children were coming up to Nika. They knew an angel when they saw one. Nika spent time with each one, all of them leaving happy, the troubled ones leaving comforted. Simon thought that should they fail to find Claus, perhaps he was sitting close to the new Spirit of Christmas. But then Nika said, "Those last two, the boy and girl. They are brother and sister. Let us just say that their parents are now on my personal naughty list. After the new year, the children's lives will improve. The lives of their parents will not." There was a fire in her eyes when she said this, a fire Simon understood and at times had felt when he taught a needed lesson to the ungodly. No, Nika was not likely to become the Spirit of Christmas, and if Claus had come to a bad end, Simon felt sorry for those who caused it.

But Claus still had to be found, and Simon had no idea how. Then another child came up to Nika. The little boy's laughter sparked something in him. He opened himself up to his surroundings and felt mostly happy people around him. Yes, they had their problems. Yes, some of them were angry at others. Yes, some were worried about things going on in their lives, but despite that, they were happy because, well, it was Christmas and it was the season to be happy.

So, Simon thought, *as the abbess said to the bishop, you're going about this all wrong. I need to stop searching for the Spirit of Christmas and use that spirit to trace it to its source.*

He began with the ice rink. Extending his senses, he reached out to the people there. There was an older couple, skating arm-in-arm for the 40th year in a row. There were newlyweds, holding each other tight as they made their first circuit ever around the rink. There were children of all ages, the cold biting into their faces as they enjoyed the feeling of flying that skating on ice was giving them.

And there were the watchers, the ones who did not skate themselves but who took pleasure in watching others.

Simon felt their joy and moved on. Children and their parents, or more often grandparents, looking at the toy displays in the various shops; the children wishing they had time to amend their lists to Santa and making mental notes for next year, the adults thinking much the same thing, the grandparents having a quiet word with a salesperson and making payment and delivery arrangements.

Simon went further, soaking in the general good feeling of Manhattan at Christmas. Of course, there were those who thought Christmas a bother and a humbug, but they were few and easily ignored.

When he was done, when it seemed that his heart had grown

three sizes that day, when he had the strength of ten mages plus two, he let the river of joy go and bade it seek its source. It flowed from him and his mind followed it.

South to Midtown, then through Greenwich and East Villages. It was drawn to Soho where it lessened, and its light dimmed as it entered Lower Manhattan. He thought maybe that was because of the 9/11 Memorial but that was not it, because it did not brighten when it crossed the bridge into Brooklyn.

It ended in an alley in Brooklyn Heights, the once powerful light of joy down to the mere flickering of a sputtering candle.

Knowing where to find Claus, he came back to himself. "It's bad, we have to go," he told Nika. "There's little time."

"Where?"

He opened his mind and showed her.

If you were in Rockefeller Plaza that day, and if you were not watching the skaters and you were turned just the right way, you would have seen a dark-skinned woman with back hair unfold ash grey wings to their fullest extent. You would have seen her embrace her companion and rise high into the air. You would have felt the wind of her passing as she flew away much faster than a speeding bullet.If you were an adult, you would probably have passed this off as some kind of a trick and wondered how she did it. But if you were a child, or had the innocence of one, you would forever remember the day that you saw an angel in Manhattan.

It takes an hour by subway to get from Rockefeller Center to Brooklyn Heights. It takes longer by cab or car. Nika and Simon arrived mere minutes after she spread her wings.

Claus was lying in a little-used alley. He was thin, his hair and beard grey. He was dressed in fading jeans and a blue shirt. The only red about him was the blood that had leaked from several knife wounds and onto his clothing. The angel ran over and cradled him in her arms.

"Nika, I held on as best I could. I knew you'd find me."

"Claus, we'll get you help. Simon here can ..."

"He's beyond my healing." Simon had seen death in many

forms. Sometimes he caused it. Sometimes he avenged it. And sometimes, like this time, there was nothing to do but accept it and wait.

Nika spread her wings. She would have lifted him up but Claus stopped her. "No, this body is done."

"Then whoever did this will suffer."

"No," Claus said again. "Find them, yes. But this is the season of forgiveness. Keep that in mind. Now, before I pass on to the Divine, use your sword. Take my essence."

"Claus …"

"You know how. And soon you'll know why. Farewell."

Claus closed his eyes but opened them long enough for one last whispered, "Merry Christmas."

With tears filling her eyes, Nika drew her flaming sword and plunged it into Claus's chest. His body gave a great heave and then it was nothing more than an empty shell.

Her sword still in her hand, she turned to Simon. "Find him."

Simon was not about to argue with an angry angel. Nor was he inclined to. He was not sure if Nika had agreed to forgive Claus's killer but he knew that he had made no such promise. Instead, he envisioned finding a portal to the Pit, dragging the killer's nearly lifeless body to it, then throwing him into the deepest circle he could reach. There were demons who owed him favors. Simon planned on calling every one of them in to ensure this person's eternal suffering.

So find him Simon did.

Blood is a part of the essence of a person, part of the song that is unique to them. And by spilling Claus's essence, his killer bound himself to his blood.

Touching what had been Claus's blood Simon asked, no, he demanded that the Universe show him where the killer was hiding. Such was the strength of his demand, the Universe complied immediately.

"Three blocks away," Simon said.

There were three of them. Two women and a man, young in

age, old in sin and experience, in the basement of a vacant house. One of the girls, Janet, was stained with Claus's blood and with his death.

By now, Simon had calmed. Perhaps it was Claus's request to forgive them. Perhaps his Spirit of Christmas was still lingering. For whatever reason, Simon decided that since long ago the Divine had declared that vengeance was Theirs, he would, in this case, let Them have it. He would remain and bear witness.

"She's yours," Simon said to Nika.

"I know."

Even with her wings folded and unseen and with her sword of fire hidden from mortal eyes, Nika was still a frightening sight. Slowly she approached Janet as Simon held the other two back.

Nika drew her sword which burned brightly as she held it before the frightened Janet. She was about to plunge it into the woman when suddenly she stopped. Holding the blade in front of her she spoke to it.

"Yes, old friend, of course. What a wonderful idea."

Then to Janet. "This will hurt you, but it will not kill you. Whatever happens after that is up to you." She thrust the sword into the young woman's body.

Her companions moved, whether to rush toward their friend or to run away, but Simon held them fast. "Stay and watch."

When Nika pulled the sword out of her, Janet fell to her knees. She let out a great wail as she realized who and what she had killed. "Oh my God, what have I done?" She started to cry and shake, the others letting her be. Finally, she calmed and began talking, not to them and not to herself but to the one now inside her.

"Yes, I see. Yes, I accept. Tell me what I must do."

Then, what once been a flickering flame of a nearly burnt-out candle flared as the Spirit of Christmas was reborn.

"Claus?" Simon asked.

"No," Nika replied. "He is now with the Divine." Then she asked the young woman, "And you are?"

"Call me Joy." To her friends, the newly named Joy said,

"Come with me."

"Why?" one asked.

"To do what?" asked the other.

"Don't be silly. It's Christmas Eve and we have work to do."

"But why us?"

"Because you're now my elves. Are you coming or do I leave you here with them?"

The three left together to save Christmas.

"Now what?" Simon asked when the two were alone.

"May I suggest a much slower flight back to Manhattan, dinner followed by a brisk walk, then midnight Mass at St. Patrick's."

"Sounds good, but let's make it Baltimore and Mass at the Basilica of the Assumption. I know the Archbishop. I can get us seats up front."

"And after that?" There was that smile again.

"I know this place called Sebastian's. They'll love you there. Have you ever had a Twisted Elf?"

The Haunted Museum

It was a few weeks into the new year. The angel Nika had returned to her divine duties leaving Simon Tombs alone. He didn't mind being alone, at least, that's what he told himself. In his long life, he had been alone more often than not. Still, he reflected, being with someone was nice, not just for the physical aspects but for the companionship, the partnership. Having someone with whom to share his life and adventures made things all the more exciting.

These things will come when they will, Simon thought, *and there's no sense in rushing them. Rushing only spoils things.*

Simon was on the sofa in his living room reading, alternating between a book on quantum magic and the latest issue of *From the Shadows.* Having fully digested her latest rat, his boa constrictor Kitty was awake and about. As she slithered from room to room, Simon realized that she was probably searching for Fel, Simon's former assistant, friend, and lover.

I think Kitty misses her more than I do. After all, Fel did give off more heat. Simon paused, remembering how much heat the reformed demon's body could give off when she was excited.

A wonder I wasn't burned to death, Simon thought as something on the floor caught his eyes.

It was a feather, grey with a blackened tip. One of Nika's. *Who would have thought angels shed so much?* He picked it up and put it with the rest. He couldn't really throw them out, that would not have been right, and one never knew when angel feathers would come in handy.

Finished with his reading, Simon considered calling Caitlin Hood. *Maybe she'll answer this time.* But before he could, his phone rang.

Speak of the devil, or rather, the detective, he thought. Looking at the caller ID, he saw it wasn't her. It was, however, a number he recognized, that of Stuart Newman.

But he's dead and in Hell, Simon thought as he looked at his phone. *At least he's supposed to be.* Simon knew that others had returned from both Above and Below, so why not him?

Stuart Newman had been the owner and operator of the Madison Museum of Antiquities. He and Simon had been acquaintances and shared a few adventures. But then Newman tried to purchase his dead father's soul from the Pit using the thirty coins Judas Iscariot had received for betraying Christ.

Simon and Fel had stopped him, Simon replacing two of the coins with US silver dollars. When Newman presented them to the demons with whom he was dealing, they believed he had tried to betray them. Shadows with red eyes and sharp teeth destroyed his body and carried his soul down to Hell.

When what was left of Newman's body was found, Simon and Fel were, of course, suspected. Fortunately for them, they had established good alibis.

Simon's phone was set for six rings before going to voicemail. On the fourth one, he said aloud, "Oh what the hell." Instantly regretting the phrase, he answered his phone.

"Hello?"

"Mr. Tombs? Mr. Simon Tombs?"

It was a woman's voice. "Yes?" Simon asked warily.

"You don't know me. I'm Beatrice Newman. Stuart Newman was my uncle. Can we meet? It's about the museum."

The museum. Before he died, Stuart Newman had implied that there were "dangerous items" in his museum, ones that, if set free, would terrorize the city. Newman's threat to do so was his "or else" to get Simon to turn over the betrayer's coin that was in his possession.

Just after Newman's messy death, Simon tried to get back into the museum to find those items and make them safe. He called Caitlin Hood and requested supervised entry. Before he could explain why,

"No way in Hell, Tombs. That museum is still a crime scene and I'm sure that you had something to do with what happened in there. There's no way I'm letting you anywhere near that place. The museum stays locked down until the court orders me to release it to the next of kin."

"I don't think you understand. There are dangerous things inside …"

"So you say. My people have been all over it and nothing happened to them."

Realizing that there was no talking to her, Simon said quietly, "So be it, Caitlin. You've seen some of the evil that lurks in the shadows. If it's your Choice to leave them be and hope for the best, then any consequences are on you. Call me if you change your mind."

She did not call back.

Simon considered a quiet break-in but Caitlin would be expecting that. he did not doubt that she had set up surveillance devices and he wasn't sure he could avoid them all without using magic, magic that might awaken the "dangerous items."

Nothing happened. Whatever danger was inside the museum remained there. Soon other events drove his worries about the museum from his mind.

Until the call from Beatrice Newman.

At Simon's suggestion, Beatrice Newman met him at Sebastian's. Meeting there rather than at the museum would give him home field advantage and he would not have to worry about a demon popping out of a damasked box.

They arranged to meet at seven. Simon arrived five minutes early, dressed to impress in a grey suit, white shirt, and a tie that had tiny, almost unnoticeable, bat-emblems on it. Beatrice was ten minutes late, arriving in black jeans, top, and jacket. With her dark hair and eyes, she was almost a shadow, making Simon wonder if she wasn't one already, possibly corrupted by something in the museum. He stood at her approach. She was tall, almost Simon's height. Up close he could see that she was well-proportioned with soft features that she had not inherited from her uncle.

Once they were seated and drinks were on their way, Beatrice got right to the point.

"My uncle's estate has finally been settled. He left me the museum and enough money that I don't have to work unless I want to. After I took ownership, I was contacted by a police detective, Caitlin Hood. In turning over the keys to the building she told me that my uncle was murdered and that you were somehow involved."

A simple statement but one that held many questions.

Simon shook his head and smiled. "Caitlin and I have had a long and … interesting relationship." When Beatrice spocked an eyebrow and gave him a certain look, Simon was quick to say, "Oh no, nothing physical. I'm not her type." *But you might be*, he thought but didn't say.

"It's just that, for some reason, when any of her cases turn weird or strange she thinks I'm involved." *And sometimes am.*

"As for what happened to your uncle, a friend and I visited Stuart at the museum the day he died. There I learned that he was dealing with dangerous forces, those from the deepest circle of Hell. I advised him against his actions. He told me that if I tried to stop him, he'd unleash some if not all of his museum's most deadly items on the city. Given the choice between your uncle and

Baltimore, I chose the city and left your uncle to his fate."

Simon's explanation was not quite the truth, but it was close enough.

Beatrice nodded. She did not sound angry when she said, "Detective Hood told me you were strange and I think she was right. But yes, I thought that was the case. My uncle was not a well man. And he was not a good man. The rest of the family had nothing to do with him. I barely knew him. I was as surprised as anyone when he left me the museum."

Beatrice reached out and touched his right arm just above his wrist. "Which is why I wanted to meet with you, Mr. Tombs. I've been through my uncle's papers. Some of them indicate just what you said, that some of the items in his collection were dangerous, and not just the antique blades and pistols. At first, I thought he was imagining things, that the "dangers" were all part of his sickness, along with his claim that his father was some sort of serial killer. If that's true, maybe madness runs in my family. Not a comforting thought."

Simon thought of the words of the Chesire Cat, "We're all mad here." To Beatrice, he said, "When I was young, a man I worked with, and never mind at what but it was something of which a certain detective chief inspector did not approve, told me that life can make you crazy, that there was no escaping it. The thing to do, he said, was to make sure you went crazy in your way and not anyone else's."

At this, Beatrice snorted. It was a delightful snort; the best Simon had ever heard. "Well, if I am going to go crazy, I don't want to go my uncle's way. But here's the thing. I've been through the museum twice, and I swear I've heard voices. Nothing distinct, just low mumblings. That's why I believe you about the magic and all that. There's more than one voice and I think they're either talking about me or plotting against me. Or I'm already mad. Which is why, Mr. Tombs, I'd like you to come to the museum. I'm going to be converting it into an antique shoppe, yes, it will be spelled like you think, people expect that. I was hoping that you would go through the museum, find the dangerous items, and either make them safe or destroy them for me.

Simon quickly agreed. "How about tomorrow morning at nine?" he suggested.

She smiled. "Make it ten. Now, I must be going."

"May I see you home?" *Now where did that come from?* he wondered.

"No, thank you." Beatrice took out her phone. "I'll call for a ride."

Ten the next morning. Again Simon was early and Beatrice late. After she unlocked the door, he said, "Wait outside. I'll find whatever's inside better without mortal distractions." And she was distracting, this time in a red top with matching pants, the red alleviated only by the same black jacket she had worn the night before. Her hair was red as well, causing Simon to wonder which was the wig, the red one or the black.

He tried not to stare, her slight smile telling him that he had not quite succeeded. Still, he was not going to ask. When she gestured him inside, he entered and closed the door behind him, leaving her outside.

Simon had come prepared. About his person were knives, amulets, and potions and oils sacred to a variety of beliefs. In his mind were wards, spells, incantations, and rites of exorcism. He had memorized these to the point where only a word or two would suffice to complete an entire ritual.

Simon took a moment to study the museum's layout, if one could call it that. The exhibits were random, identified only by a note card. A 14th-century book of prayer lay next to an advertisement for a late 1800s New Orleans bordello. Sometimes, though, things lined up, like the 18th-century Spanish sword and mask which had been placed next to a slouch hat, black cloak, and paired .45 semi-automatics from the 1930s.

Things did talk to him, one or two items per room. There was the damasked box he had thought of earlier and which he had long suspected of malevolence. *Open me and I will grant you great things*, it seemed to say. An empty diamond-patterned bottle which once contained an 1823 Prosecco now held swirling smoke. *Any woman you desire, any time you choose, any way you want.* Another smaller bottle seemed to shout, *Drink me*, without making any promises. There was an enchanted blade (*One scratch and your opponent will die*) and a flintlock pistol that promised its ball would always find its target's heart.

Trapped spirits all, condemned to their prisons and forced, maybe, to do their possessors' bidding. Simon could only imagine their effects on the museum's visitors. Those blind to the supernatural would feel a slight unease and a little excitement. The more sensitive, however good and kind their nature, would be tempted. Most would reject this temptation while some would covet the object, furtively look around, and wonder about the quality of the museum's security.

Simon dealt with these objects one at a time. Standing in front of the item, his hands almost touching it, he'd say a prayer then recite a ritual of release, sending the trapped spirit to whatever fate it deserved. From many came a cry of pain, *No, do not do this. Save me and I will serve you however long you live*, or something like that. From a few came a simple *Thank you* as they ascended to their reward.

Simon paused and let his senses fill the first floor. The damasked box was just that, a box and no more. Nothing swirled inside the Prosecco bottle, now filled only with the memory of wine long gone. The smaller bottle was silent. The weapons were still deadly, but only in the ways their creators had intended.

Simon cast a general spell, one designed to reveal any evil or trapped spirit that he may have missed. There were none. The first floor was clear.

Satisfied with a job well done, Simon was a bit disappointed. Stuart Newman had promised, well, threatened, to unleash Hell upon Baltimore if Simon did not meet his demand for the last coin of the Betrayer. But the objects he had encountered posed only individual threats and would have been no danger to the city as a whole.

Had Newman been bluffing? Simon was upset at the prospect. Not only at having fallen for Newman's bluff but also at the thought that had he seen through it, Newman might still be alive.

Simon turned toward the back stairway that led upstairs to more exhibits and Newman's office, the office where Simon had switched coins and where Newman had tried to buy a soul with false treasure.

The stairway was lined with portraits of people who had died centuries ago. They were important in their time but now mostly forgotten. Newman had not even bothered to identify many of them. Simon paused at each one. None seemed haunted or possessed and none of the eyes followed him. A few of the eyes, however, had tiny holes out of which one could look. He imagined one of these portraits hanging in the bedchamber of the lord of the manor. The lord would be having his way with a lady not his wife while his wife, hiding in a secret passage, witnessed his adultery through his own eyes.

I wonder, thought Simon, *if afterward she confronted him. If so, did she kill him, threaten to leave him, or ask, "Why have you never done* that *to me?" Whatever* that *was.*

But that was mundane drama, and not what Simon was looking for. He wondered if Beatrice knew about the spy portraits and, if so, did she plan to charge more for them, then watch the papers to see if the purchasers or someone close to them died of violence.

I better not bring that up. There's enough violence in Baltimore without my inadvertently adding to it.

No sooner did Simon step onto the second floor than the reek of demons assaulted his psychic senses. Here there were several demons housed in a variety of ways. Housed was the correct word, for none of those he sensed were trapped in their containers. They could leave them at any time, but only to return to the Pit. As an eternity of voluntary confinement was preferable to one of hellish pain, they remained of their own free will, waiting for someone to pick them up or, worse, purchase them. Then, once claimed, they would be free to possess their owners and wreak the havoc that was their nature.

Strange that I didn't notice these before. No doubt Stuart shielded and controlled them. When he died, the shields fell, the control weakened, and they grew strong. Caitlin, you should have let me in when I asked.

Simon sensed the demons stirring. They were aware of him as much as he was of them. He took a moment to study the items in the room. Among them — a plague demon in a glass hand, waiting to spread its virulence. With this plague, there would be no incubation period, no vaccinations, just quick, painful death that would spread over several states before the demon was forced back to Hell. A stoppered bottle containing an infernal djinn who would grant its wishes in ways that would damn its "master's" soul. The bottle would then be passed on, claiming soul after soul. A Tarot deck lay on a table, its cards cursed to foretell only doom and containing the power to bring it about.

There were paintings on the walls, each of which depicted one of the Deadly Sins. They were arranged, as best as one could in a squarish room, so that they formed a seven-pointed star. Own one of these and you own the sin, or rather, the sin owns you.

Why did Stuart have these? Hubris, I suppose, the belief that he could control them and keep the world safe from them. He was right, until the end. The question is, what do I do with them? Oh well, when in doubt, attack.

All along, the demons had been as focused on him as he was on them. He had felt them probing him, searching for weakness. His wards held and they did not find any.

Feeling the eyes of the Seven on him, Simon stepped to the near center of the room, attracting even more of the demons' attention.

"For those of you who do not know of me, I call myself Simon Tombs. I am Lord Mage of Fairie and the tamer of demons. I have sent many of your kind back to the Pit and I have dared Hell itself in order to rescue repentant souls. I do not fear you because, just as you might know me, I know you. I know you all. I have read the Book, the first book that was carved soon after the Fall of Man. It contains the names of all those cast out of Paradise. I've read and memorized the names and can pronounce them in the First Language. Do any of you dare challenge me?"

Simon paused to judge the effect. The djinn had stopped swirling, the lesser demons withdrew into their containers. On the walls, six of the Deadly Sins now seemed to be avoiding his gaze, with only Pride daring to look at him.

Time to go all in. "What about you, Pride? Shall I speak the name that was old when Sumer was young? The name you were known by in the streets of Uruk? Do you want to return to the Pit the hard way?"

Pride's eyes turned away.

"I can destroy you all. I can speak your names and send you screaming to the bottom of the Pit. You will fall for a very long time, your pain increasing as you descend. When you do strike bottom, there you will face your masters, the ones who led the First Rebellion. Their pain is the greatest of all, and they will gladly share it with you."

Simon paused, took a breath. "But I would not wish such pain even on creatures as evil as you. So I will be merciful. Depart from this world on your own. Resume your places in Hell as best you can. And while you suffer there, consider what you did to deserve that suffering. Who knows, you may come to regret your sins. If so, on that day I may come to save you."

All was quiet, then it was as if there was a great rush of air, one that Simon felt in his soul. Outside, dogs howled and cats screeched. Birds flew random patterns and Beatrice all but collapsed from the worst headache she'd ever had. Then, all was once again quiet.

Simon looked around the room. The bottle was empty, the djinn gone. The Tarot cards were a pile of ash. The other items were in similar condition. The paintings on the wall were, however, resisting him .

"Go, now," Simon commanded as he drew a knife with an obsidian blade. "The Knife of Ammit, Devourer of Souls. Should I slash your canvas homes, she will feast on you for hundreds of years. And when she is finished with you, she will void you out to even worse punishments in Hell."

Within minutes, the canvases were blank.

Simon opened his mind and scanned the room. It was clean, with no trace of evil. Going into Newman's old office he found it likewise clean. Except …

In one corner, there was a small shadow that should not have been there. As Simon watched, it grew to the size of a Rottweiler. Then red eyes appeared and it smiled with great sharp teeth.

When it spoke its voice was one of razor-blade fingernails on a chalkboard. "I have been waiting, Simon Tombs. Ever since you used Stuart Newman to cheat us out of the coins, I have been waiting. I knew you'd be back. I had expected you sooner, but you let that police woman keep you away. But no matter, for what are a few years compared to the eternity of my existence. An eternity you will now share. And do not think to bluff me the way you did those lesser demons. For their weakness, they will suffer along with you."

Simon knew this demon as a creature from the Pit. One of the most damned. One whose name was in the book. As it advanced on him, Simon pronounced a name in a language that was as old as the Fall of Man.

The Pit demon did not have time to scream as it collapsed in on itself and returned to Hell.

Looking at where it had been, Simon said, "I wasn't bluffing, you dammed fool."

The job done; Simon went outside where Beatrice was waiting. On seeing him, she ran into his arms.

"Oh, Simon, I was so worried. I heard, I felt …"

He returned her embrace. "Not to worry, whatever was in there is gone now."

Beatrice held him tighter. "Oh thank you. How can I … would

you like to see me home?"

Her intent was obvious, the "rescued" maiden giving the gallant knight his earned reward. He was tempted, but then he remembered that the woman in his arms may have spoken with demons. He gently broke the embrace.

"Why don't we take things slow? How about we start with lunch at Fortuna's of Fells Point?"

The Guardian

The demon who called herself "Fel" had once been an angel. When the Morningstar rebelled against the Divine, she had but a moment to choose whether to serve and protect humanity as she had been commanded to do, or to follow Lucifer.

She chose poorly and was cast into the great pit of darkness that was Hell, there to suffer with the rest of those who had rejected the Divine.

How long she suffered she did not know, for there is no time in the Pit. She came to regret her decision. But just as there is no time in Hell, so there is no escape. Not for one like her.

She was a minor demon, fit only to share her suffering with those humans who chose Evil over Good and who had turned their backs on God. She had no name and no one on Earth ever summoned her. But she, along with all the demons of Hell, knew when such summonses were about to occur.

She was near one summons when it came. But as happens in Hell, something went wrong. The summons was interrupted. As the gateway to the mortal world began to close, she again had but a moment to make a choice.

This time she chose wisely and escaped the Pit into the custody of a man who called himself Simon Tombs. He could have sent her back but did not. Instead, he became her teacher, her friend, her companion, and her lover. As they fought against the Darkness that was in the world, she fought against the darkness that was still within her. "Guardian Demon" she called herself.

Then Hell came, not for her but for Simon. Standing back to back, they fought as long as they could. When it became clear that they would be overwhelmed, he set her free.

"You who are known as Fel," he said, even as the two fought back the ever-growing horde. "As the one who summoned you, as the one who holds power and mastery over you, I release you from any and all obligations to me. I give you leave to walk freely upon the Earth until such time as you are called to your final fate. May you find peace and joy."

Seemingly betraying him as she had told him she would, she left him but she did so with a purpose. Humbling herself before the Divine, she begged Them to save Simon. They agreed, just as she agreed to the price of Their help.

There is a bridge over the Great Chasm between Paradise and Perdition, one that repentant souls may cross. A Guardian is needed to protect them on their journey. Do you accept?"

"For how long?" Fel dared to ask.

"Until your penance is complete. Until We have forgiven you. Until you have forgiven yourself. We ask again, do you accept?"

Fel accepted. No longer a demon, but not yet an angel, she became the guardian of the bridge between Heaven and Hell.

Bearing wings of white and a sword of fire, she fought back the demons and protected the repentant from them. And none had yet been able to stand against her.

But it was not enough for her to merely guard the Bridge because she knew when a soul repented. A small part of Hell became brighter and she could trace that brightness as it moved closer to the Bridge. Sometimes it went out, the soul having succumbed to despair. Sometimes it was snatched by demons and sent to deeper regions to begin its journey again.

How can I help them? Fel wondered. *I can't abandon my post. And I definitely can't move the Bridge.*

Suddenly it was as if Simon was there beside her. "Remember *my* bridge," he seemed to say, then he, if it was him, was gone.

Simon had told her the story. He had an obligation to a soul in Hell, a *repentant* soul. Using the connection between them, Simon imagined a cord tying them together. The cord became a rope, and the rope a bridge. Simon then crossed that bridge and saved the soul. It was the first soul he stole from the Pit, but not the last.

If Simon can do it, I can do it, she decided. *After all, I have an obligation to save them if I can.*

The next time the brightness appeared, Fel used this obligation and imagined a thread tying her and the soul together. The thread became a cord, and the cord a rope. The rope was all she needed. Pulling on her end, she drew the Soul of Light toward her.

Reeling them in was physically exhausting and something kept her from drawing the soul all the way. *As it should be,* she realized. Redemption must be fought for. So she watched as the soul fought its way past the demons that would destroy it. Once it came close enough, she fought for it and saw it safely over the Bridge.

"Thank you," it said as it passed into the Paradise she was still denied.

Then, inside her head, she heard Simon's voice say, "I knew you could do it. Good job."

She knew it could not be Simon, but then angry demons, deprived of their prey, rushed the Bridge, and any thoughts she had were lost in the thrill of battle.

Elsewhere, in the deepest circle of the Pit, the collective known as Satan thought, *She must be stopped. This guardian demon, this Fel, must fall.*

Blink of an Eye

I

My name is Johnson Leonard. And this is likely the last post of mine anyone will ever read. Yeah, I know, a bit dramatic, but I have to put the story out there, in the hope that someone will believe that not all stories are made up and there's danger behind urban legends and myths.

I don't know where we started drinking that night, some place on Frederick Avenue near the city, I think. We kept drinking as we headed west, finally ending up in some bar in Ellicott City called the Blink Man Tavern.

"What's a Blink Man? Maybe they meant the Blind Man." Freddie said.

"Or the Blond Man?" countered Amy. "I could use one of them, a big, blond man with a big …"

"Naw," said one of the locals, cutting her off. Amy could be a bit of a flirt and the more she drank the flirtier she got. Right then she was eyeing Wallace. He's new to our company, Charm City Technology, and yes, he is big and blond. This was his first time on our monthly Friday blowout. We pick a direction and a designated driver and stop at whatever bar or tavern looks friendly and inviting.

The rule is one round per place. That keeps things from getting out of hand and Amy in her clothes. I was driving that night, limiting myself to one beer every third stop, with iced tea at the other two. That kept me well below the limit even if I did have to pee a lot.

But to get back to the local, he was a small, thin man, maybe in his fifties, and he introduced himself as Columbo.

"Like the TV show?" Bruce asked.

"No, I don't like the TV show. But my parents did. One night it was on and they stopped paying attention to it and started paying attention to each other. Anyway, I was born about nine months later and so they named me Columbo."

"Could have been worse, man" Dantay told him.

"How?" Columbo asked.

"They could have been watching *Maude*."

We all laughed, including Columbo. Once we stopped, he asked, "You really want to know why this place is called 'The Blink Man?'"

I did and said so. I looked at my group of happy drinkers. They were nodding. I checked my phone. It was pushing eleven. Time for a story and one last round.

"Last call, people. Order up. You too, Columbo."

We got our drinks. He got his. Then Amy said, "Tell us a story, Lieutenant." The look he gave her told us that he'd been called that before. But he had ordered the good stuff on our tab so he didn't say anything. Instead, he started his story.

Damn, I wish we'd never stopped there. Damn, I wish Freddie and Amy hadn't made those stupid jokes about the bar's name. And damn, I wish Columbo had picked another place to drink that night.

"It all started early 1900s," Columbo said. "That's when the hole was blasted through the mountain to let the train go through instead of around. The trestle spanned the Patapsco River and led into the Ilchester Tunnel. Nothing wrong with that. It was the way things were done in those days. Use force to take the easy way instead of the hard way. Guess things haven't changed that much, have they? Anyway, this time it looks like they woke something up."

"Like what?" Freddie interrupted. "Something like the Hell House altar?"

"Patience, young man. If you ever watched my namesake, you know it takes him a bit to get to the point. And yes, I've watched them all, but only once with my parents. Their giggling just freaked me out. And no, nothing like the 'Hell House altar.' No murders there, no black masses either. That was more of a party spot. More than a few virgins were sacrificed on that altar but only in a good way." Columbo paused, took a sip, and added, "Or so I've been told."

His smile said otherwise.

"No, this was something else, something darker, something maybe not of this world. Or maybe something asleep and buried that the blasting woke up – Peeping Tom, the Blink Man, the Flickergeist. And I don't know where that name comes from, for old Tom has never been known for looking through windows. You have to go looking for him."

His glass was empty. We refilled it and he went on.

"It's said that if you stand at one end of the Ilchester Tunnel around eleven p.m. and stare down to the other end without blinking until midnight, you'll see him. He'll be tall and thin, his clothes and hat blackened by the soot of all the trains that have passed through the tunnel. But that's not all. Once you see old Tom, you can't unsee him. The first time he's at the end of the tunnel. Blink, and he's closer. Blink again and he's closer still. And no, you can't turn or walk away. You're trapped in a for-keeps staring contest. You try not to blink, but Tom's been playing this game longer than you or anyone else. Sooner or later you blink, and he's closer. And then he's right up on you, so close his long eyelashes are brushing your face. If he blinks, you win and go free. If you blink, it's all over."

"What happens next?"

Columbo answered Wallace with a shrug. "Don't know. Nobody who lost ever came back. Maybe he throws your body in the Patapsco. Maybe he eats you, or you just disappear. Or maybe, you take his place and there you are, waiting for the next fool."

Story over, Columbo put his glass down hard on the table. We thanked him for a story well told, paid our tab, and left. I was pulling my hatchback out of the parking lot when Freddie observed, "You know, the Ilchester tunnel's not that far from here."

I was tempted. For some reason, Columbo's story got to me. But it was past midnight. So I found Frederick Road and headed back to the firm. There we crashed in our cubicles, got some sleep, and woke up sober enough to get in a few hours' work before driving home.

That should have been the end of it. But, damn me, it wasn't.

I couldn't help myself. Maybe it was the story or the way Columbo told it. Or the seeming implausibility of the whole thing. Or the "no one knows what happens next" ending. I had to know more.

I spent Saturday afternoon searching terms like Flickergeist, Blink Man, Ellicott City legends, and crap like that. That, of course, led me down the rabbit holes of urban legends, Maryland mysteries, and cryptid lore. None of it helped. It was all myth and speculation. I needed more and I could think of only one way to get it.

That night found me on Frederick Road looking for River Road. Once I found it, I went on to Ilchester Road. I parked under the bridge and climbed up to the tracks and the tunnel.

Trusting that my phone was right about the trains not running at night, I made my way to the south end. I checked the time. Right at eleven, I stepped into its mouth and looked forward. Trying not to blink, I stared toward the other end. My world was soon reduced to a small patch of light surrounded by darkness. I heard night noises, somewhat amplified, and I saw things, maybe. I lost my sense of time. Had I been there ten, twenty, thirty minutes? More? I might have stayed there until daylight filled the tunnel or I caught an early northbound train the hard way.

Common sense slowly returned. *What am I doing here?* I asked myself as the absurdity of my actions became clear. *I'm in a train tunnel waiting for a ghost that likely doesn't exist. If he does and I see him, he'll kill me, maybe, within several blinks of my eyes. Time to leave,* I decided, very, very glad I had told no one else about my trip.

And there he was. Peeping Tom. And he looked just like Columbo said he would — tall and thin, dusty black clothing and hat. The storyteller had forgotten to mention the blood-red eyes.

Did I test the legend? Despite the rational part of my brain screaming "NO!" of course I did. With Tom and me locked in a stare, I deliberately blinked and as I did, heard chimes. An oncoming train? No, trains don't chime. Phone alarms do. I had set mine for a minute past midnight to let me know it was time to leave.

Silencing the alarm, I looked down the tunnel. No Tom. I blinked again and again. Still no Tom. According to the story, by now we should have been up against each other, his eyelashes tickling my face in one final, fatal stare-down.

But there was nothing except something to add to the legend. The Blink Man is afraid of loud noises. If you go to see him, make sure to set an alarm.

I let out a sigh. I had challenged death and won. But where had Tom come from in the first place? I figured it out on the drive back. Stare at nothing long enough and your brain fills in the blank with something. In my case, it was the Blink Man. I had expected to see him and so I did. So much for the legend of Peeping Tom the Flickergeist. So much for my compulsion.

On the way back to the city and sanity, I switched on a music streaming channel. Some new group called the Retrogrades came on. Their bit was very old songs with very modern beats. I didn't catch the title but, damn, the words stuck with me:

"Yesterday upon the stairs,

I met a man who wasn't there.

He wasn't there again today,

Oh, how I wish he'd go away."

There was more to the song, but I didn't hear it. I quickly changed the disturbing music to nature sounds.

At the time, I thought it just a strange coincidence. Now, however, who can say?

I mostly forgot about Peeping Tom, train tunnels, and men who weren't there until two weeks later when I went to Annapolis to see a client. I parked in a garage off the Duke of Gloucester Street. When I returned to my car I saw … him, Tom. He was like before — tall, thin, dark, and sooty. He was at the far end of the second level of the garage, his red eyes shining in the darkness. Our eyes locked. *Don't blink,* I told myself as we held each other's gaze. Two minutes, maybe three went by. Then Tom smiled. I blinked and he was gone. A few more foolish blinks. Nothing.

Somehow I made it to my car. I don't remember doing so. I sat there, frightened and wondering. How? Why? This was Annapolis, not Ellicott City. And a parking garage is not a train tunnel. *You're marked,* my mind's voice of unreason told me. *Back in the tunnel, Tom marked you. You escaped him through luck, but he's come to claim his own.*

No, I countered, *it was a trick of the light, a flashback to a scary moment.*

Just the same, you better practice not blinking.

I sat in my SUV until I felt sane enough to drive. I hit the FM and a singer told me that he'd be watching every step I took. I shut it off.

Six days later, I was walking from work back to the ten-hour meters in front of St. Vincent's. It was growing dark and I had my Baltimore City radar working, watching for anyone coming toward me, listening for footsteps behind me, a hand in my jacket pocket holding my not-even-close-to-legal stun gun. (He came at me with it, Officer. Somehow I got it away from him and shocked him. Will he be all right?)

I walked up President Street, crossed Fayette, turned right on the short block to Front Street and there he was, a half block away, standing on the sidewalk in front of the church, a dusty shade amid the lengthening evening shadows.

I had been practicing. I could stare without blinking for about five minutes. Again Tom smiled, or at least parted his thin lips to show his rotting teeth. He then nodded as if to say, "Let's see what you've got."

What I had was my hand on my stun gun. If a cell phone startled him, what would 1200 volts do? I walked forward, thinking, *Let's end this.*

Tom waited, watching my approach. Neither of us blinking. Then,

Bong!

The Westminster chimes of St. Vincent's started sounding out the quarter hour, surprising us both.

I blinked and almost shocked myself. I looked for Tom. Of course he was gone. But then I heard what sounded like the voice of a very young man say, "Not this time."

Not that time, but the next time, two days later the face I saw in the mirror was not mine. I quickly turned, thinking he was behind me. He wasn't and when I turned back, it was my face that stared back. But this close I remember seeing a young face behind the dirt, and very long, very beautiful lashes.

I did not go to work that day, or the day after, or today. Instead, I've written my story and posted it on every social platform I could. The posts are time-delayed. If I can, I'll cancel them tomorrow. I don't think that's going to happen.

It's night, almost eleven, a good time to take a walk, to meet a man who isn't there. I'll have my stun gun in my pocket, but I don't think it will do me any good when Tom's beautiful long lashes are brushing my face. I can now go without blinking for ten minutes. I don't think that will be long enough.

||

Johnson Leonard's final message to the world went out on schedule to be shared and reshared. Downloads of Retrograde's entire catalog doubled, then tripled, then dropped off as more well-known musicians put out their own arrangements of poet Hughes Means's *The Little Man Who Wasn't There*. Some claimed it was a hoax, one review called it, "above-average Lovecraft-styled horror fiction." Still others embraced it wholeheartedly as a brave revelation of the things that were not there. They cited the disappearance of Johnson Leonard as proof.

The Baltimore Police Department issued the following statement: "In response to a request by Ms. Amy Hudson of the local IT firm Charm City Technology, who was concerned for Mr. Leonard's health and well-being, patrol officers performed a wellness check at his apartment. Mr. Leonard's apartment was intact with no signs of forced entry, ransacking, or foul play. No indications of Mr. Leonard's present whereabouts were found. A missing person report has been filed."

Simon Tombs read Johnson Leonard's final post. He, more than most, believed it to be true and considered involving himself. It was his nature to investigate such occurrences. But he decided to wait until the hoopla and hysteria surrounding the whole business died down.

So instead, he devoted himself to the new work by Biblical scholar Ora Russo. The title of their book was *The Words of the Christ*. The first chapter discussed the only known writing of Jesus, his "scribbling" in the dirt in front of a suspected adulteress and her accusers. What these words were the Evangelist doesn't say. Mx. Russo speculates that whatever they were, they might have been remembered and later written down by one of His disciples. They further argue that there were probably other "hidden writings" which form the basis of a "secret knowledge" passed on from generation to generation.

"Nothing can be kept secret for that long," Simon said to his boa constrictor Kitty, who was at that time gently wrapped around his leg. "Someone would have talked. I'll have to ask Judas the next time I see him."

Simon was debating whether to continue his reading — he was curious as to what Mx. Russo thought this secret knowledge was and where it might be found — when the phone rang.

"Mr. Tombs, my name is Amy Hudson. I don't know if you remember me but I was a server at Sebastian's some time ago."

He did remember and told her so. Then Simon remembered where he had last read her name. "You're concerned about what might have happened to your co-worker Johnson Leonard. I take it you're not satisfied with the efforts of the BPD."

"No, I'm not, Mr. Tombs. They did a quick search of hospitals, lockups, and the morgue then it was file and forget. I remembered some of the strange things that happened at Sebastian's, like when that woman crashed in and you helped her and the police came and you took off your shirt. I really remember that last part. So I decided to call you. Hope you don't mind?"

"No, I don't. I was going to look into it later. But I guess I'll start now."

"Oh, thank you, Mr. Tombs. Do you need to talk to me about it? We could meet at Sebastian's, or maybe at the Blink Man, or I could come up to your apartment."

Leonard was right about Amy being a flirt. She had been when she worked at Sebastian's. She made big tips that way. He considered her offers, both suggested and possibly implied. Amy was not unattractive, he recalled. She had long brown hair and a decent figure. But right then she was worried and vulnerable and Simon was not one to take advantage. Besides, he was not yet over Fel and Nika.

"Thank you, Amy, but I think I got all I need from Johnson's post. If I need more, I'll call you or one of your co-workers. Would you text me their numbers? Thank you."

"What's your first step?"

"Research. There were one or two things in Johnson's post that bothered me. Goodbye for now. When this is all over you, me, and the Charm City crew can meet at Sebastian's for some Pepper Specials and Hotter Chocolate."

Yes, research, Simon thought after Amy hung up. *Lots of research. But first, a trip to the Blink Man tavern.*

Thanks to the now well-known legend of Peeping Tom the Flickergeist being attached to it, the Blink Man tavern was packed, even early on a Wednesday evening. A $20 contribution to a server's college fund snagged Simon a small table in a far corner. He ordered a white wine then looked around for Columbo the storyteller. He found him at a large table against the far wall, surrounded by people buying him drinks so he'd tell them all about Peeping Tom.

Simon was surprised when he saw him. "Oh, so that's what happened to him," he said to himself just as the server brought his drink.

"To whom, sir?"

"Never mind." Parting with another ten, Simon said, "When he's free, please tell, eh, Columbo I'd like to buy him a drink."

The small, thin man was about to tell yet another group of curious drinkers about the Blink Man and how the poor unfortunate Johnson Leonard had met his fate when the server passed on Simon's message. Columbo looked toward Simon's table, excused himself, and went over to him.

"Simon Tombs, well I'll be. You know, even in a Polo shirt and slacks, you still manage to put the rest of us to shame, even most of the women."

Just then the server came over. He had already gotten thirty off this customer and he was determined to earn more by giving him the best service he'd ever had.

"My friend Columbo will have a double scotch, top shelf, higher than the top shelf if you have it. And bring me another glass of white."

The server left. Simon looked at his table companion and said, "So, Charlie Cape, I understand it's Columbo now. The last time we met, it was in a bar in Frederick called the Snally and the Dway. You were cadging drinks talking about the county's cryptids. You called yourself 'Hawkeye' then and told your marks you were conceived during an exceptionally intense episode of MASH."

"You know how it is, Mr. Tombs. You do what you can to get by."

"I know, Char…Columbo. I take it you've read the last testament of Johnson Leonard?"

Columbo waved his arms to encompass the bar. "Hasn't everybody? Look around you. This place has never been so busy. And there's a place up the street that renamed itself 'Peeping Tom's.'

And a lot of the shops on Main Street are selling Blink Man tees, caps, and even those googly-eyed glasses. Business has never been better."

"Damn shame a man died to make it so. Or did he? Johnson isn't hiding somewhere counting his share of the take?"

"No, it's nothing like that, Mr. Tombs. That guy messed with Peeping Tom now he's gone where all the others went. I feel bad about that, but I'm just a storyteller."

"Are you sure? You're not pimping for the Flickergeist, are you?"

Columbo managed to look worried and offended at the same time. "Mr. Tombs, Simon, you wound me."

"No, but if you're lying to me I might. But never mind that. Now tell me what you didn't tell the police."

"I told them everything, Mr. Tombs. Swear to God I told them everything. I mean, I felt terrible but I had nothing to do with whatever happened to that guy."

"And yet you keep telling the story that killed him."

"Like I said, you do what you can to get by."

Simon handled Columbo a fifty. "Here, take the rest of the night off." Then he settled with his server, adding a very nice tip to the over-priced drinks, and left. He had research to do.

The internet first, checking newspaper archives — Library of Congress, Maryland State Archives, Newspaper Archives — and online journals. Then field trips, first to the Miller branch of the Howard County Library, then to newspaper offices and the warehouses where they stored their microfilm records and sometimes yellowing copies of the old newspapers themselves.

The viaduct over the Patapsco River that led to the Ilchester Tunnel was built in 1903. The first sighting of a "flickering ghost" was 1905. There were numerous articles since then, usually around Halloween or when the bridge was featured in a story. Sometimes "Peeping Tom" was mentioned as a sidebar to the unexplained disappearance of a local.

Simon went back, narrowing his search to events between

1903 and 1905. He looked for drownings in the Patapsco under or near the bridge. And reported falls or jumps from the bridge. Any other drownings would leave the river haunted, not the bridge. Murders? Not as many as one would expect, Howard County wasn't Baltimore nor was it mystery fiction involving a local detective.

Of the murders that had been reported, there were no shootings, stabbings, or other violent assaults inside the tunnel or maidens tied to train tracks by blackhearted, mustache-twirling villains.

That left accidents and again these were few. The one that stood out was the death of thirteen-year-old Benjamin Wyatt who disappeared in the Fall of 1904. The article mentioned that Wyatt, known to friends and family as "Benny," was a "disturbed" young man and, if found, should be approached cautiously. A few days later, Benny's body was found by a B&O track inspector. He had been struck and run over by a train.

What happened, Benny? Simon asked. *Was someone with you and did they escape or leave you? Were you murdered and your killer used the train to cover their tracks?*

Simon winced at this accidental pun and continued reading going backward from Benny's disappearance.

He found articles on the front pages of the Ellicott City News and the Howard County American. These were public service warnings about a "prowler" in the area who was "peeping" into windows at night. He had been reported spying on women in various stages of undress and on couples "in intimate embrace." Readers were advised to take "appropriate steps" to avoid being watched.

The newspapers repeated the articles several times, each repetition more and more critical of the police who had so far failed to catch "Peeping Tom." The last mention of the voyeur was two days after Benny's body was found. An article in the News merely stated that the police had reported the threat of the Peeper ended. No details were given.

"It could have happened like that, Kitty," Simon said to his snake as he watched the Three Stooges on TV while she lay fat and happy after finally digesting her latest meal of alley rat. "I suppose we'll never know. Unless I ask him of course."

Simon went back to watching Larry, Moe, and Shemp. By the time the short was over, he had part of an answer to one of his questions.

"You know, Kitty, with one refinement that might work. If it doesn't, I guess I'll find out what happened to the Blink Man's victims."

The following night found Simon at the mouth of the Ilchester Tunnel. Closing his eyes and slowing his breathing, Simon quieted his mind and sent it forward, searching for things that were other than natural. Immediately he reeled back. There was death there. Not bodies buried in the ground or bones lying amid rocks that had fallen to the side but death throughout. Steeling himself, Simon probed deeper, letting out a sigh when he found no trapped spirits.

"So that's what you did with the ones you killed," he said out loud, not quite sure if the Flickergeist was there to hear him. Maybe it took the ritual to summon him, or did the Blink Man use the ritual to tire his victim? "You have the tunnel absorb their bodies and you feed from the tunnel. What did you do with Johnson Leonard's body? Absorb it directly? Or did you just throw it down a sewer? But it's time to finish this."

Simon's innate time sense told him that it was just eleven. Having no desire to stare into the tunnel for an hour, he shouted, "Benjamin Wyatt, also known as Benny, by your name I call you. Appear now!"

If this is someone or some thing other than Wyatt, Simon thought, *I'm going to look very foolish. And I hate appearing foolish in front of a ghost. It's embarrassing.*

Simon did not have to wait. One second the tunnel's other end was empty then, in a blink of Simon's eyes, there he was — tall, slender, clothed in a dusty darkness. His face was thin and his eyes glowed red. He was just as Johnson Leonard had described him.

Simon faced the geist without the weapons Leonard was planning to use. If he had used them in their final encounter they had done him no good. So Simon's phone was turned off and, since he had never needed a stun gun, he didn't own one. No, on this adventure Simon was relying on something he had picked up at a convenience store and a trick he learned watching TV.

"We're bonded now, aren't we?" Simon asked, taking care not to blink. "That's how you found Johnson Leonard. Once your eyes locked, you could leave your prison and find him anywhere."

Very deliberately, Simon blinked and the geist shifted 300 of the tunnel's 1400-foot length.

"What was it like, Benny, growing up 'different' than the other boys? They bullied you, didn't they?"

Blink. Another 200 feet.

"Then your body started changing in ways you couldn't understand. It was not something you could talk over with your folks, and you had no friends to clue you in."

Blink. 200 hundred feet, halfway there.

"Then you started peeping. And you got caught. Probably by one man at first, a husband or father. Then his hue and cry set the pack on you. They chased you and hunted you like an animal."

Blink. A third of the remaining distance, call it 250 feet.

The next time, Simon thought. *Or the time after.*

"You knew about the tunnel. Everybody did. You hid here. Did they find you, beat you to death, and leave you for the train? Or did the train do the job all by itself?"

Blink. The next time the geist would be within arm's length. And the time after that, his long lashes would brush Simon's face. Simon prayed that it would not come to that.

"And you were trapped here. And started killing. Why? Hatred? Revenge? Hunger? Or did it just feel so damn good, better than the feeling you got peeping through windows at naked women and what you did afterward? Or did you do it *while* you were peeping?"

Simon blinked and as he did, put on the convenience store

mirrored sunglasses he had purchased earlier that day. Hoping the geist was confused by seeing himself instead of his victim's eyes, Simon stepped forward and threw a two-fingered poke at Benny's eyes.

And Benny blinked.

Thinking *Thank you, Moe*, and, letting out a quiet sigh, Simon said gently, "You flinched Benny. You lose, I win. And as the winner, I command you to depart this place for whatever awaits you in the next. And may God have mercy on your soul."

Behind his mirror-shades, Simon blinked and Benjamin Wyatt, Peeping Tom the Flickergeist was gone.

Again Simon sent his mind out. Except for the residue of the long dead, all was quiet.

On his drive home, Simon decided to let Charlie Cape continue telling his story. People would soon lose interest and "Columbo" would have to find another bar, another cryptid. As for Amy, all he would tell her, over drinks at Sebastian's, was that he had slain the monster and avenged her friend. He'd forgo the customary hero's reward. He'd keep the mirror-shades. One never knew when belief would raise another flickergeist.

The Wine of Cana

Roland Grant checked the locks of his Talbot Street house one last time. The deadbolts were thrown. The windows were locked and the bolts of their interior bars secure. Convinced he was safe, at least for the night, Roland climbed the stairs to his bedroom.

The arrangements had all been made. *One more week*, he thought, *then it will be all over*. He could not wait. He was surprised that he could sleep. How many years had it been? So many had died. Now it was just the six of them.

Strange I haven't heard from any of them since the online meeting last month, Roland thought as he got into bed and under the heavy covers. He liked his house, it suited him, but damn if it wasn't cold in the winter. None of the windows sealed properly. Roland had thought about installing thermal windows but changed his mind after considering how many ways the wind and the cold could creep into his old house. *But then again*, he reflected, thinking about the others as he pulled up a comforter, *we all know where and when. And what's at stake. It's not likely that any of them will miss a once-in-a-lifetime opportunity. No, not a once in a lifetime, once in many, many lifetimes, never to be repeated*. Roland dozed off, trying to imagine what the experience would be like.

And awoke to a noise coming from downstairs.

The house settling, he told himself. *Old houses make strange noises. Probably the furnace.*

But neither the house nor the furnace made sounds like someone climbing the stairs. Slow, deliberate steps, a creak after every second or third tread. Loud, heavy steps as if the intruder wanted him to know he was coming.

He quickly got out of bed, his feet automatically finding his slippers. Taking a mental survey of his bedroom, he could think of nothing he could use as a weapon.

A burglar, Roland thought. Why not? A house on the water, one set back from the others? He was surprised it hadn't happened sooner. He'd go back to bed, pretend to be asleep, and let them take what they wanted.

Two more steps, one more creak.

There was no landline in the bedroom. That was downstairs so the ringing wouldn't wake him. His cell phone was turned off for the same reason. Ten seconds to turn it on. Time enough to call for help but not for it to arrive.

Another creak. The loud one just before the top step. The intruder was near. Glad he'd never bothered with a passcode, Roland swiped on. He hit the phone icon then called the only number he thought could help him. It was not 9-1-1.

I hope you're in town like you said you'd be, Roland thought just as the door opened.

Like Roland Grant, Simon Tombs was awakened by a loud noise. It was not an intruder. They tended to fall from a great height, wind up in the Baltimore Harbor, or have some other strange, inexplicable accident befall them. The last was found naked inside the gym of an all-girls school. When he tried to explain what happened to him he found that he couldn't.

When Simon's phone went off, he reached out to the other side of the bed, found it empty, and sighed. "I should be used to that by now," he said to Kitty, not even sure how much the boa constrictor could hear him or if she was even in the room. He looked at his caller ID, saw who it was, and answered,

"Judas, why are you calling so early in the morning?"

The voice that answered still carried the traces of the Judean town in which he had been born. "Morning? But the sun hasn't risen. Oh, right. Never could get used to that. I need your help, Simon."

"Of course. Where are you?"

"In a rented car driving towards some place called Edgemere. I'm looking for an old house off, of all things, Cuckold Place Road." He gave Simon the address. "Can you meet me there?"

"What's this all about?"

"I'm not certain, but I'm sure I'll need you. Park around back."

Sometime after that, Simon parked his car next to a red Toyota. Judas was outside the car waiting for him. He was shorter than Simon's six feet and had the darkened skin of someone who had spent much of his long life, a life much longer than Simon's, in the Middle East. Because of the weather, his coat was zipped up, hiding the rope scar around his neck.

"Have you gone inside yet?" Simon asked after he got out of his car.

Judas shook his head. "Door's locked. I've been waiting for you to do that thing you do."

Simon nodded. "Anyone see you drive up?"

"No, I don't think so. Late night, quiet area. Didn't see any lights. You?"

"Even if they did, one car looks much like any other these days. In the dark even more so. Now then, let me remind the back door of its obligations."

Having been convinced that Simon's key was the right one, the door opened into the kitchen. That led to a dining room which led to a sitting room that led into a small entry and hallway. Across the hallway was a large room that had been given over to storage. Opposite the front door were narrow stairs that led up.

"Call out to him," Simon said.

"Are you sure?"

Simon nodded. "Anyone here probably heard or saw us pull up."

"And are likely waiting upstairs to surprise us."

Giving Judas a pleased smile of anticipation, Simon said, "Too bad for them. Now call out. Grant does know your voice?"

Judas nodded and yelled. "Roland, are you there? It's Judas. I brought a friend. We're coming up."

No answer from above. No other noises either. Simon and Judas slowly climbed the stairs, the creaks of the treads betraying them.

There were two rooms at the top. The door to the one on the left was open. They tried that one first. It was a large room. To the left of the king-sized bed, a dead man lay on the floor.

"Roland Grant, I presume?"

Judas nodded.

"Don't come in any further," Simon cautioned. "Back out into the hallway."

As Judas did so, Simon, not wanting to add any more of himself to the murder scene than he already had, stood still and searched the room with his eyes. No signs that the furniture had been searched. No disturbance other than the dead man at his feet.

The downstairs hasn't been ransacked either, Simon thought. *So it's murder and not burglary.*

Judging from Roland's wounds and the bloody bat on the bed, he had been beaten to death. Blood stains and castoff told Simon that the killer had started swinging almost as soon as he entered the room. Broken body. Broken face. Broken hand. Broken phone. The killer had struck while Roland was calling for help.

"Judas, when Grant called you, what did you hear?"

"Enough to know he was in trouble."

"Specifically."

"I heard someone say, 'The spare key right where it was supposed to be.'

"Male or female?"

Judas closed his eyes, thought back. "High-voiced male, low-voiced female. Can't say."

"What then?"

"Roland said, 'You, but I thought you were ...'"

"Then the first voice again. 'The others did too.' That's all. Listen, Simon, Roland is gone. We should be too in case someone called the police."

"If they had, they would be here already. We have time." Using his handkerchief, Simon picked up the bat. "Come here, take this."

"But that's the murder weapon."

"I know, but it won't do the police any good. The grip is wrapped with a kind of tape that doesn't hold prints. The blood on it will come back to the victim. All the police will get is confirmation that the bat was used in the killing and we need it more than they do. Here, take this too." He bent down, retrieved Roland's cell phone, and gave that to Judas. "It's smashed up but the police's forensic people might be able to establish the last number called. Your number, my friend. They'll check his call logs. Your phone's not in your current name, is it?"

Judas shook his head. "It's not."

"Good, lose it. Hope you've got everything backed up."

"Fine, can we go now?"

"For someone who's more than two millennia old, you're very impatient. Let's see. The killer locked the back door when they left, delaying discovery of the body and creating a locked house mystery for the police. We'll leave the back door open and unlocked. Hopefully, someone will call about it." Simon stopped and thought for a moment. "Maybe a small fire to attract attention," he said more to himself than Judas. "No, that could easily get out of control. I know. Judas, before you dump your phone call in and report a prowler.

"We're done here. There's a Late-Nite Eats on Eastern Avenue. I'll meet you there."

It was the time between the night owls and the early birds so the Late-Nite was not that crowded. Simon ordered Belgian waffles with a large chocolate milk. Judas got the Dundalk breakfast along with a large coffee.

"Do you think anyone saw our cars?"

Simon shrugged. "Probably, but, as I said, all cars look alike these days. There was a time when you could tell a Ford from a Dodge from a Chrysler but not now. And CCTV is more of a TV plot device than anything else."

A sigh of relief from Judas. "Good. Now I can understand you taking the phone, but why the bat?'

"Violent acts form bonds between the victim and assailant. The bat is the link. I can use the blood on it to track the killer. And finding the murder weapon in the suspect's possession is more helpful to the police than finding it on the crime scene. I mean, what's the killer going to say? 'I left that on the crime scene?' Now, Jude, tell me a story, and make sure you start it right."

"Okay, a long time ago in a Galilee far away, there was a wedding feast in the town of Kafr Qanna, best known today as Cana. The Boss and those He had gathered, including me, attended as escorts for His mother. She was, in a sense, a mother to us all, and that's what we called her – 'Mother', or rather, 'Ima' and not "Woman" as that oaf John wrote. The bridegroom was a relation, a cousin I think. You know the rest. They ran out of wine, which may have been our fault, we did drink a lot of it, especially Rocky and his brother Andrew. Mary saw that the bridegroom was embarrassed and asked the Boss to help. He was … reluctant. It may have been because He wasn't ready to go public or He was still coming to terms with His Divine nature. But Mary was His mother and He was a dutiful son. What was He going to say, no?

"Let me tell you, those stone water jars were big, each holding about twenty to thirty gallons. And there were six of them. Do the math."

"120 to 180 gallons, I would think."

Judas nodded. "That's about right. And all six filled with the best wine I've ever tasted." Judas paused in his story, as if savoring the memory. "We didn't drink it all, although, believe me, we tried. We did take a couple of bottles away with us. So did some of the other guests. The bride and groom kept the rest.

"Over the years, make that centuries, there were rumors about the Wine of Cana, of how some of it survived. Most of these weren't true. But some were. Now and again a true bottle would turn up. There were stories about men killing for one and women trading what virtue they had left for a single cupful. Sort of goes against the Boss's teachings but that's humanity for you.

"Now fast-forward to thirty years ago. An amphora, sealed with wax, was found not far from where the scrolls were dug up. It was smuggled out of the country and purchased by a group of wine connoisseurs. And that's where I come in."

"You were one of them?"

"No, I couldn't afford the buy-in. But I was working in antiquities then." Simon gave Judas a look. "Well, why not? I was alive when most of the antiques were new. I was called in to authenticate their purchase. I told them that the bottle itself was genuine as far as the place and time. As for the wine, if it was still fresh when opened, it was the real thing. After all, wine He made wouldn't go bad, would it?"

"But they didn't open it, did they?"

Judas shook his head. "No, they each wanted all of it, not just a cup. It started as a tontine, the bottle placed in a vault in a Swiss bank, to be turned over to the last person standing. Two months ago the six survivors voted five to one to meet, open it, and drink the last of the Wine of Cana. Which is where I come back into it. My price for the authentication was to be there when the bottle was opened, and to have a small sip of it.

"The opening is a week from yesterday. I came to town early to see you then meet with Roland. The rest you know."

The two sat quietly for a while, finishing their breakfasts in silence. Finally, Simon said, "Tell me again what you heard over Grant's phone."

Judas did.

"The spare key …I thought you were … The others did too. That's what was said?" Judas nodded. "Were what?"

Before Judas could answer Simon said, "'I thought you were dead' comes to mind. As for the 'others' thinking so as well …"

"My God!" Judas exclaimed. "Whoever it is faked their death and killed the rest of them."

"Possibly, you did say that men had previously killed for a taste of the Wine. Why not now?"

"Agreed, and as the sole survivor they'll be the only one

present when the wine is delivered."

"When and where?"

Judas shook his head. "Roland knew, they all did. But he didn't tell me."

"So we find the killer and ask them."

"And how do we find them?"

"For that, we have the bat."

It was just after dawn. Judas watched Simon remove the baseball bat from the butcher paper in which he wrapped it when they left the house on Talbot Street.

"You just happened to have that in your trunk."

Simon smiled. "Jude, my trunk is a collection of 'just in case' items – rope, twine, canvas bags, magnets, weights, not to mention more arcane items like, well, best I don't mention them."

The two were in Simon's study. He spread the paper out on his desk to protect it.

"I thought you had a workshop for this sort of thing."

"I used to. It's still recovering from the fires."

"What fires?"

"The ones from the Infernal invasion. Oh, it was glorious. There were demons and devils. Fel betrayed me then saved me, bringing a small army of repentant souls with her. When it was all over, she kissed me and flew away. I haven't seen her since."

Simon's blue-gray eyes misted for a moment and there was sadness in his voice as he said, "But enough of that. We have work to do."

Taking a cotton swab, he wet it and collected some blood from the bat. Then he tied the swab to a string, letting it hang tip-down.

"Grab that tablet from the bookcase. Thank you. Now put on gloves, move the bat aside, and lay the tablet in front of me." When Judas had done this, Simon said, "Computer, open Channel D."

A female voice replied, "How may I help you?"

"Open mapping program, five blocks centered on this location."

When the map of Baltimore appeared, Simon dangled the

swab over the screen. "Computer, attend." Simon said some words in old Gaelic and the map began moving on its own.

"You're cyber-scrying. Nice."

"It's a trick I picked up reading a book about a police detective who fights monsters. You can learn so much from fiction. I may weaponize DNA next."

Simon and Judas watched as the map's image moved north, following I-83 until it came to Schwann Rd in Hunt Valley, Md. It stopped over a sprawling hotel-convention complex.

"They were supposed to tear this down, but someone decided there was life in the old girl yet. They bought it and renovated it. Which is good for us. No one notices guests at a hotel unless you dump piranha in the swimming pool."

"Simon, you didn't."

"Of course not. Just something else I saw on TV. Computer, close Channel D."

Simon took another blood swab, wrapped the bat in fresh paper, and handed the package to Judas, saying "Take charge of this." He then smeared the swab over the face of a directional compass. "Once we're inside the hotel, this will lead us right to the killer's door. After that, well, we'll see, won't we? When we're done, we'll leave them unconscious and in possession of a murder weapon."

Simon's plan worked almost to perfection. No one questioned them when they walked into the hotel, Judas carrying the bat inside a black case. The compass led the pair to a second-floor room where a "Do Not Disturb" sign hung from the exterior handle.

"They're likely in there," Simon warned. "Be prepared for some rough stuff."

"That's one thing I'm good at," Judas replied. "Are you going to do the door thing again?"

"No, I thought I'd knock and see what happens. When the door opens, rush in and knock down whoever answers."

Putting on a pair of thin gloves, Simon knocked. No answer. He knocked again with the same result. Grasping the outside handle, he pushed and the door opened.

They entered slowly, paused and listened, and heard nothing. On one side of them was a closet, on the other a bathroom. Judas checked it and made sure it was empty. Passing into the main part of the room, they saw the body of a man lying on the bed furthest from the windows.

A wine bottle was on the table between the beds. A hotel-supplied glass tumbler had spilled its contents over the deceased after it had apparently slipped from his hand.

"Recognize him, Jude?"

"Etienne de Bodard. French native, now living in Newport, Rhode Island. He was part of the original group. He supposedly died three months ago. I guess he got better."

"Well, maybe he was only mostly dead. Would he have known about Grant's spare key?"

Judas shook his head. "As far as I know they had no personal contact. What are you thinking, Simon?"

"I'm thinking you should count the glasses. There should be four of them."

After a moment, Judas said, "There's only three."

Simon nodded. "Two of them were working together. De Bodard probably did the dirty work. The other brought a bottle of wine to celebrate Grant's murder, a bottle doctored by injecting poison through the wrapping and the cork. One drank, the other pretended to. One died, the other walked away, taking the glass they used with them."

"So what now? Maybe whoever did this is the sole survivor unless some of the others are in on it. Which others I don't know. Simon, can you do your swab magic and find the poisoner?"

"No, blood is life, and in violent death, it cries out. Poisoned wine? I don't think it's enough."

Simon poured some of the poisoned wine into the glass de Bodard had used. He corked the bottle, intending to take it with him. Then Simon threw the case containing the bat on the other bed, then stepped back. *The killer will be found*, he thought. *The police will be called. They'll search, find the bloody bat, and match it to Roland Grant.* He looked at the dead body. *They may take the easy way out and figure that de Bodard killed Grant in a rage, regretted it, and killed himself with poisoned wine. Or they may not. They may worry about the missing bottle. That part is now out of my hands.*

Extending his senses, Simon found that there was no one in the outside hallway. As they left the room, Simon closed the door so it locked and flipped the door sign to "Please make up this room." *Forgive me*, he thought, thinking of the poor unfortunate who would find the body.

"Where was the meeting place?" Simon asked Judas, who shook his head.

"We didn't get that far. And by now whoever killed Roland and Etienne could be anywhere and, unless you can make some magic with the poisoned wine, we have no way to trace them."

"Think back to that first meeting, when you authenticated the amphora, did Grant appear close to anyone back then."

Judas put his head back and closed his eyes. "Give me a minute. I can remember things that happened 2,000 years ago but not the name of my last lover. And that was less than a year ago. Plus the 1960s and 70s are just one big blur. We all met in … London, in a boutique hotel in Chelsea. There was someone, a woman. There were several women in the group but one came in with Roland." Judas was quiet as he thought some more. "They left together as well."

"Did they seem close in a more-than-friends way?"

"Let's see. When they arrived, they moved their chairs a bit closer to each other. When they left, I think she said something about bringing the car around. So yes, more than friends if I'm remembering right."

"Do you remember her name?"

It began with a D, no, a C. Camile, Clare, maybe Charlie. Not, not Charlie. She was there and definitely female but she was wearing a man's suit that had been tailored for her figure. Very androgynous, very alluring. I think we were all panting after her. Except for Roland and … Clare, definitely Clare. Funny how thinking of one woman can help you remember the name of another. Except for my last lover's. I wish I could remember her name. I'd give her a call and see how fondly she remembered me."

"If at all."

Judas sighed. "So true. But what does a woman Roland was with thirty years ago have to do with this?"

"Maybe they were together long enough for Grant to tell her where he kept his spare key."

"And she passed this information on to de Bodard and that's how he knew where it was. But how does it help us?"

"I don't know. Let me work on it."

As Simon had predicted, a swab made from the poisoned bottle did not help, the map on Simon's tablet not moving as the swab hovered above it.

"Let's get dinner," Simon said, giving up on the cyber-scrying. "Then drinks at Sebastian's. Maybe something will occur to me."

Over dinner, they talked about everything but the Wine of Cana. They were in Sebastian's where they continued avoiding the topic as Simon waited for something to occur to him.

"I'll have a Hotter Chocolate. What about you, Jude?"

"I'll stick to wine."

When Judas said this, Simon stared at him for a moment then started laughing, and laughing, and laughing. With the other patrons staring (but not the staff, they were used to Simon acting strangely), he laughed a full three minutes before he calmed down enough to say,

"Jude, I'm an idiot."

"I know. I started telling you that seven names ago, three of mine and four of yours. Why are you an idiot this time?"

"Because I just realized the answer is literally staring me in the face. Just as I am staring into his."

Judas realized that Simon was staring at him.

"What? Me?"

"Yes, Jude, you," Simon said and explained how.

Neither Simon nor Judas mentioned the Wine until the day before it was to be delivered when Simon said, "The meeting place has to be somewhere in this area, or at least within driving distance. Why else would Grant have you come to Baltimore? Plus de Bodard stayed in the area. And so, presumably, did his killer. It's time."

In Simon's apartment, Judas lay on the bed in what had been Fel's bedroom. He was barefoot, his head propped up on two pillows, and his hands folded on his chest. The room was dark except for a single candle.

Simon spoke from behind the candle.

"Close your eyes, think back to the beginning. The Wedding Feast. You're there with Him. He has changed the water into wine. You've drank it and it is the finest wine you've ever tasted or ever will taste. And because He made it, a small part of it will always be with you."

Simon's voice is quiet, almost a whisper, and hypnotic. Judas finds himself drifting back across the centuries.

He's there, in Kafr Qanna. He's been served a cup of the new wine. He takes a sip, wary that it's a joke of some kind. Yeshua always had a strange sense of humor. But it's not a joke, it's not water but the best wine there ever was. He gulps it, then goes for another cup, and another, and still more. And no matter how much he drinks, he cannot get drunk. Not from this wine.

That's when he knew that this man was Someone special. Not from the other signs, not from the preaching. From the wine.

"Judas." Simon's voice comes from a distance. It pulls him away from the Feast. "The wine is in you. Do not think of where it was but where it is. Think of who is with it. The messenger. For now, the wine is his, not to drink, but he is its guardian, its protector. He is closer to the Wine than anyone. Do you feel him?" Judas nodded slightly. "Then tell me what he's thinking?"

"He's thinking of a woman. She's not his wife. She and her husband live in Pennsylvania. The messenger's wife is in Bern. He's meeting her in … Annapolis. He's in a hotel room. He's waiting for her. He's thinking of what they will be doing when she arrives."

Simon blew out the candle and put on a light, causing Judas to blink several times. As his eyes adjusted he noticed that Simon did not seem to have that problem.

"Can you still feel the wine?" Simon asked.

Judas paused, searched for its feeling. Yes, it was still there, his mind a little heady from the thought of it. He nodded.

"Very good. Get your shoes on," Simon told him. "Once I get a few things we might need, we're driving to Annapolis."

On the way, Simon said more to himself than Judas, "A B&B in the historic area is too expensive for a one or two-night stand. And B&Bs are more personal and someone might remember them. The outlying hotels then."

They were on Route 50 when Judas suddenly said, "I feel the Wine. It's close. Take this exit."

When Simon pulled onto Riva Road, Judas directed him to a hotel where Simon parked next to an airport rental car. A few spots away was a Honda with PA plates. Soon they were standing outside of a second-floor room.

"The Wine's inside," Judas said. "Should we knock?"

"No, let's surprise them."

Simon took an old hotel key card he kept in his wallet for just such an occasion and swiped it through the reader. There was a click as the security catch disengaged and the door opened.

Simon and Judas moved quietly so as not to awaken the lovers who were sleeping the sleep of the just after. A muttered spell from Simon made sure they would remain asleep. That done, they turned on a light and searched the room.

"Found the Wine," Judas whispered, indicating a small, wheeled, metal suitcase.

"And I have his wallet and identification." Simon looked through the wallet and found a slip of paper on which was written, "Annapolis Tavern, second floor. 11 a.m. local time."

Simon smiled. Using a piece of hotel stationery he left the

messenger a note.

"Herr Mueller, Don't worry about the package. It will be delivered as scheduled. If you call the police or attempt to interfere, the photos I took will be sent to her husband, your wife, and your employer. All the best."

Judas read the note. "You didn't take any photos."

"He doesn't know that," Simon replied. "Now let's get a room for the night and tomorrow we'll play this game out."

It was a quarter to eleven the next morning. Simon and Judas were sitting at a table in the second-floor dining room of the Annapolis Tavern. The room was used primarily for events and had been rented for the meeting.

Then Clare Gideon walked in and closed the door behind her.

Affecting a Swiss German accent, Simon said, "Other than this gentleman, you are the first to arrive. May I have your name, please."

"Clare Gideon."

Simon pretended to consult a paper he had before him. "Ah, yes, Ms. Gideon. And this gentleman, for today let's call him 'Jude,' was your authenticator. He's here as per agreement."

From the look on Clare's face, it was clear she wanted to but didn't dare ask Judas how he learned about the meeting. Instead, she asked Simon,

"And you are Herr Mueller?"

"No, I am not," Simon replied, dropping his accent. "My name is Simon Tombs and I am, by nature and inclination, a busybody and a righter of wrongs."

Clare stood as if to leave. "You may leave if you wish, Ms. Gideon, but we'll keep the Wine, and you'll have killed all those people for nothing."

She sat back down. "What makes you think I killed anyone?"

"Ms. Gideon, we are all adults and none of us fools. You wanted the Wine for yourself. With Ettienne de Bodard's help, you killed the survivors of the tontine. I'm guessing it was you who voted against this meeting. But no matter. Neither Jude nor I are police, and neither of us plan to stop you from having a taste of what I've been told is a very fine wine. Now, shall I open the wine or would you prefer to do that?"

"Why don't you pour?"

Simon picked up the suitcase and carefully placed it on the almost three-hundred-year-old table. Breaking the seals, he opened it and took out a wooden box. This too was sealed. He opened it and removed the bottle.

It was an amphora of a size that would easily hold a liter and a half. Simon then took out three glass tumblers. If Clare noted their resemblance to those from de Bodard's room she did not remark on it.

"Ms. Gideon, Clare, before I break the seal and open this bottle, please consider this. To drink the Wine of Cana after killing so many people to obtain it is, well, a sacrilege and an insult to the One who changed it from water. My advice is to walk away and leave the Wine behind as a penance for your sins. After that, seek forgiveness and absolution."

"Are you crazy, Mr. Tombs? You only want the Wine for yourself. Besides, I have buyers waiting to pay at least a hundred grand an ounce for a taste of this. I'll have the first taste and the last, and between that collect over four million dollars. I'll even be generous and let you two have a taste. Now, break the seal and pour."

Judas watched as Simon opened the bottle that had first been sealed over two thousand years ago, then opened and resealed the night before. Like with most things, Simon Tombs had a talent for removing and replacing seals so that no one could tell he had ever tampered with them. Opening the bottle in their room, Simon replaced its contents with wine he had taken from de Bodard's room, topping it off with some of his own.

"Are you certain we have to do this, Simon?"

"There's no other choice, Jude. We have no evidence. It's the only way to get justice for the others."

"The others are past justice. The Boss would have forgiven

them, whoever he, she, or they are."

"Only if they were sorry. And I don't think that's the case here. Don't worry, they'll be asked the Question and given the Choice."

This is an execution, Judas thought as he watched Simon pour out the wine.

No, it's not, another part of his mind argued. *He warned her from the start, told her that he was a righter of wrongs. He used glasses from the hotel where she had killed de Bodard as another warning. And I doubt if she's noticed he's wearing gloves. Finally, he advised her to walk away. What did he call it? The Question and the Choice?*

Still, it was all he could do to keep from sweeping the glasses from the table then grabbing and smashing the amphora. Let her walk away thinking the wine had been destroyed. Instead, he sat silently as Simon filled Clare Gideon's tumbler.

"Still fresh," Clare said as she watched Simon pour. "Guess that authenticates the contents?"

She took a sip. "Very nice," she said, then slowly drank the rest, savoring each drop.

"And now you may have your .... Wait, what's wrong?" she asked as the poison she had used on de Bodard began to take effect.

"You chose … poorly," Simon quoted as he and Judas watched Clare Gideon die.

When she was gone, Simon said, "Leave the bottle and the glass. Put everything else in the suitcase. If the police are as sharp as they're supposed to be, they'll connect the poison and the glass to de Bodard's murder. That should keep them busy for a while."

"What about us?"

Simon smiled. "We were never here. And I can prove it."

Back in Baltimore, Simon and Judas were sitting in Simon's living room talking about nothing in particular while trying not to stare at two 750ml bottles containing the rarest wine in the world.

Finally, Simon said,

"We can't drink it."

"Not after killing someone for it."

"It's not that, Judas. I feel no remorse for what we did and if there's a new stain on my soul it's a small one. No, that Wine requires a very special occasion, and for the life of I can't think of any occasion worthy of it."

Playing with Fire

Humpty's was a bar in Federal Hill. Named after the owner's father, it was a nice place to drink with a retro county, soul, and pop theme. It did not have live music, but the old-style juke box played a steady mix of Top-40 hits from decades long past.

"Love the One You're With" was playing softly when Eddie Marks walked in. Eddie was a dealer in rare stamps and coins from Cleveland who was in Baltimore for a convention. The show had closed for the day and several people had told him that Humpty's was a nice spot to spend an evening and maybe pick up some company for later.

Eddie took "Love the One You're With" as a sign, for he was of the firm conviction that "Out of town didn't count." Never once did it occur to him that maybe his wife Brenda believed in much the same thing, that what she did when he was out of town didn't count either.

Taking a seat at a corner table, Eddie ordered a beer. "Whatever you got on tap," he told his waiter Brian. After he did, he looked over at the bar. Two male bartenders. And all male waiters. *Whatever happened to waitresses and barmaids?* he asked himself as he wondered if Humpty's was one of *those* places. But he relaxed after he scanned the crowd and saw a nice mix of friends and couples. It was then that he saw her.

She was tall and slim with pale skin and red hair. Somehow their eyes met and she smiled at him. Eddie smiled back, amazed that this good looking woman would even notice him. He pictured her as a high school senior, her height allowing her to lead her school's basketball team to victory. He had a sudden flash of her in the shower after the game, washing the sweat from her naked body.

Suddenly, he wanted her and knew he had to have her.

Catching Brian's eye, he called him over. "That woman sitting against the far wall, the tall redhead. Would you please give her another of whatever she's drinking with my compliments?"

Brian gave Eddie a knowing look and said, "Of course, sir. And nice choice."

He watched nervously as Brian brought the drink to the woman, then pointed in his direction. She smiled at him and raised her glass in a "Thank you." Hoping and wishing, he raised his back at her.

Hopes and dreams sometimes come true, for no sooner had he put his glass down than she picked hers up, left her table, and slowly walked towards him, her unencumbered breasts swaying beneath her top.

As Eddie stood at her approach, he knew what she was seeing — a man old enough to be her father, thinning brown hair and a "dad bod" that his carefully tailored clothing did its best to hide.

Still, she smiled at him and asked, "May I join you?" Her voice, friendly yet sensuous, gave all sorts of meaning to her question.

"I was hoping you would. Please, have a seat. I'm Eddie, Eddie Marks."

He didn't usually use his real name but he needed this woman to know all about him.

"Nice to meet you, Eddie. I'm Brady."

They talked. Eddie told her about his being a rare coin dealer and a little about the convention. Brady seemed interested but told him very little about herself. Finally, after another round of drinks, he judged it was time and invited her back to his hotel.

Brady smiled, said that was a wonderful idea, and quoted him a price.

I should have known, he thought, but, enthralled, he knew he could not leave without her.

Back in the hotel room, Brady called him "Daddy" and begged him to make passionate love to his "little girl." He went with the fantasy. They coupled furiously and after she gave him what he wanted, she took what she needed.

Ten minutes later, Brady was sated and left the bed. As she dressed, she looked down at what was left of Eddie.

How easy they are, she said to herself, thinking of the ones she'd had before Eddie. Shivering in lustful anticipation, she thought of the ones she'd have in the future and bade what was left of her victim farewell.

"I hope it was as good for you as it was for me."

🍷

When the man walked into Sebastian's, Simon Tombs could tell he was a police detective. He dressed like a detective. Shoes comfortable enough to wear all day while mostly standing up. An off-the-rack suit, nothing too flashy so as to avoid notice and not too expensive because the BPD's clothing allowance had not kept up with inflation for the past decade.

I really have to have a word with the mayor about dressing his police better, Simon thought. *Who was it who said the only real crime was dressing poorly? But would the public trust cops who were too well dressed? Not that they trust them all that much now.*

Simon's table was against a wall, positioned so that he could see everyone who came in but they could not immediately see him. He watched as the detective stood just inside the door and scanned the room, mentally comparing the faces he saw to the description in his head. He started on his left. Simon was seated to his right so he had time to study the detective before the man located him.

I know him. Detective … Charm. A good name for a man who works in Baltimore. One of Caitlin's strays, I think.

Charm was a large man, almost as tall as Simon. But a slight weight problem somehow made him look smaller. *A decent suit would hide that better,* Simon said to himself, still thinking about clothing the police force. He was considering the practical applications of a two-piece Kevlar suit when the detective spotted him and came over.

"Good evening, Detective Charm. How may I help you?"

"She wants to see you, Tombs."

Charm spoke in an almost whisper, a technique Simon knew as a means to make sure people paid attention to what he was saying. Or it may have been a throat injury that never healed right.

"By 'she' I take it you mean Detective Sergeant Hood?" Charm nodded. "Please, have a seat. Would you like something to drink or eat?" The detective declined both offers. "Caitlin knows where I live and the places I frequent. Since she's sent you, I can only assume this is work-related. Her work, not mine." He stood, nodded at Murphy the bartender to put his unfinished drink on his tab, and asked Charm, "Crime scene or headquarters?"

"Not HQ. And the scene was yesterday. It took her a while to finally decide to call you in."

Charm's use of "finally" intrigued Simon. "Lead on, Detective Charm. Let's see what sort of problem Caitlin has for me."

Charm took Simon past police headquarters to the Eastern Avenue Diner . It was a 24-hour place with breakfast anytime and a menu only slightly shorter than a novella.

Sergeant Hood was sitting in a corner booth. Papers, folders, and a cup of coffee covered the table.

Charm walked Simon over. "What'll you have? Coffee, soft drink, something stronger?"

"Sweet tea will be fine."

Charm brought Simon's tea then took up a guard position two booths away.

Since he was there at Caitlin's invitation, Simon waited for her to speak. While he did, he thought back to the last time they had seen each other. It was the end of a serial killer case. They were in a parking garage. Angels and demons were involved.

Finally, Caitlin took a sip of her coffee and said, "They say this stuff keeps you awake. My nightmares do that. I'll admit, Simon, the whole Heaven, Hell, and the knowledge of Good and Evil threw me. I shut down for a while. Took some leave. It didn't take me long to realize that despite it all, there were still killers to be caught. So I came back. Not that the brass were glad to see me. That last case, the Ripper one and how it played out, made them so nervous they were hoping I'd take early retirement. Well, I didn't. So they gave me the runts of the litter to work with."

"Like Charm. I remember reading about him in the papers. Nothing good."

"Screw the papers," Caitlin snorted. "They never have anything good to say about the BPD. Granted, Charm did have his problems — a questionable shooting, accusations of overtime fiddling, some missing evidence."

"So why keep him?"

"Because Simon, I see Good in him. How about you? I heard you and Fel …"

Simon shrugged. Fel was not a subject he was comfortable discussing. So he smiled and said, "Like you said, Heaven, Hell, Good, Evil. One night they all came together. When it was over we parted ways."

"And if she came back someday?"

"I still could manage a smile." More than that, he thought, but he wasn't going to tell Caitlin that. "Now, what's this problem you've finally decided to call me in on?"

She handed him photographs taken at the scene of Eddie Marks's murder.

"Hardcopy, Caitlin? I thought everything was digital now."

"Most are, these aren't. Too many cops and prosecutors with access. Look them over and you'll see why." Simon took his time with the photos, especially those showing Marks's near-mummified condition. "Look familiar?" Caitlin asked after he gave them back to her.

"The husk plague. It hit the East Coast a few decades back. Before my time."

"Your time? Or Simon Tombs's time?"

Simon ignored the question. "It's not the husk plague."

"How can you be sure?"

"The person responsible for that is dead and in Hell."

"I see. Care to elaborate?"

"No. Now, how many deaths were there before this poor bastard's?"

"Two in the past eight weeks. All in the city. The Medical Examiner is holding the bodies, all male by the way, pending further examination."

"Any signs of recent sexual activity?"

"Yes. But no match on the DNA except for the victims."

"Those two found in hotel rooms as well?"

Caitlin nodded. "The first one and Marks in the Baltimore Albion. The other in the Blue Point at the end of Pier Six."

"Is that the one with in-room movies, vibrating beds, and mirrors on the ceiling?"

The detective nodded. "Tacky but it brings in the convention crowd."

"All three here for conventions?" Caitlin nodded. "Any CCTV?"

"None yet, Subpoenas are pending. When they come in I'll have one of my squad check the videos. We'll probably only get the stuff from the lobby cameras."

"And of course, you're checking the nightspots around his hotel."

"Of course," she replied, a little irritated at Simon's question. "How about you stick to magic and let us do the police work?"

"Agreed." Simon looked around the diner. "So why here instead of downtown?"

"The brass are thinking about the husk angle and that scares the hell out of them. They're hoping I fail and scared I'll succeed so they hover, pry, and ask annoying questions. Here I can work undisturbed."

Simon took his time studying the photographs from the Marks scene. "Can you get me copies from the other scenes?" Caitlin handed him a large, manila envelope. "Thank you." He looked at those just as carefully. Three bodies drained of all fluids to the point of desiccation. "Charm was right. You should have called me sooner."

"I know, but I was told specifically not to involve you. Another reason we're here."

"Are they still upset about what happened in Brewer's Hill? That explosion was not my fault and, anyway, the house was haunted."

"What can you tell me, Simon?"

"Well, there was this ghost and she was giving the men in the house strange, pleasurable, yet painful dreams."

"I mean about Edward Marks and the other victims."

"Only that there are going to be more. Three in two months indicate a feeding cycle of two to three weeks."

Caitlin took a deep breath and slowly let it out as her fears were confirmed. "Feeding cycle? So is it a … vampire?"

"No, at least not the one I know. I'll find and ask him. Maybe he'll have some ideas as to who is hunting in his territory."

Vampires in Baltimore. Of course there are, Caitlin thought. *And Simon knows one of them. I don't know why I'm surprised. I should be used to the weird by now but it just keeps getting weirder.*

Simon said something that broke up Caitlin's musing. "Sorry, what was that?"

"I asked, aside from murder and shepherding the BPD's lost sheep, how are things going for you? Are you seeing anyone?"

Caitlin nodded. "A traffic cop of all people. She works in Accident Investigation. We met over a fatal hit and run."

"Congratulations. I hope it works out. After you warn her about me I'll take you both to dinner."

"Fat chance of that. It's too soon and I don't want to scare her off."

Detective Charm came over. "Time we got back, Sarge. The lieutenant radioed and wants to see you."

"Sure thing, Terry. Simon, you need anything else?"

"Not a thing, Caitlin. I'll let you know what I find out."

Caitlin left, leaving Charm to drive Simon home. On the way

back,

"Tombs?"

"Yes, Charm."

"I don't have to tell you that we're playing with fire here. I wouldn't want the sarge to get burned. She gave me a chance when no one else would. My last chance."

"Yes, she told me. She said that you were worth saving, that there was good inside you."

"She's good at that, telling good people from bad."

"More than you know, Detective."

Bartleby's Café was on Charles Street just below the monument. Its owners had taken over a used bookstore and converted it into a refuge for night owls. It did not open until an hour after sundown. It closed just before sunrise. It served good food at cheap prices. Not having a liquor license, Bartleby's offered a variety of non-alcoholic beverages, although the wait staff looked the other way if a patron wanted to freshen up their drink. As did the beat cops assigned to patrol the Charles Street corridor. They knew how things worked and would do nothing to disturb the ambiance or threaten their twenty percent police discount. It was there, after trying two other such places, that Simon found the vampire.

"Good evening, David," he said. "You too, Robert. May I join you?"

David and Robert were a couple. David was a vampire. Robert was not. When Simon sat down, Robert excused himself and found a place at the coffee and juice bar. He knew a little about Simon and did not care to know anymore.

"How are things going?" Simon asked, looking over at Robert.

"Ups and down, like any couple. It's better now that we can share a bed. There's a company in Maine that makes fabric from soil. I now sleep on sheets made from my native earth. I have pajamas as well, a gift from Robert for when we travel."

"And he doesn't mind when you …"

"Have to feed? No. He understands I can only bleed him every few weeks. As for the rest of the time, I have willing regulars. I find them in places like this. For them, it's exciting. For me, it's simply satisfying my appetite." David paused and took a sip of something that looked like tomato juice but probably was not. "It's different with Robert."

There was a brief quiet between the two men. David had shared his private thoughts and feelings and Simon had no wish to break the moment.

After a minute or two, David said, "Go ahead, you know you want to."

It was a game between the two, a game David always won. This time, however, Simon thought he had him beat.

Taking a handful of loose change from his pocket, Simon tossed it on the table.

As soon as the last coin came to rest, David said, "A dollar twenty-seven." Then Simon's mental *Gotcha* was wiped out by, "Plus a Canadian dime. Simon, that's cheating, but I'll still let you buy the next round."

"That's amazing."

"Yes, I know. That's why I've always said that puppet on television is one of the most accurate portrayals of my kin."

"How do you think he feeds?"

"How else, off the hand that's sticking up his butt. A bit kinky but I've heard of worse. Now, what brings you out at this hour? Couldn't you sleep or is it … something else?"

"Something else, I'm afraid. I need your help." Simon handed him an envelope with three photographs in it, one from each crime scene. "I warn you; this is definitely worse than kinky."

David looked at the photographs and turned as pale as his dark skin would allow. He quickly put them back in the envelope.

"This is not the work of any of my kin," he said in a shaky voice. "The police don't think …"

"Not anymore. I assured them otherwise. And no, I did not

tell them anything specific about you. And no, I was not followed."

"Good. I have lived in Baltimore all my lives, the one before and the one after, and do not want to leave it. And then there are the others to think about. There are five of us now. I have the city; the rest have divided Baltimore and Anne Arundel counties among themselves."

"I know."

"Of course you do. We are at peace and I would hate for anything to disturb that, or them."

"I'll do my best but the sooner this … creature is stopped, the better for all of us."

David drained his glass of "juice" and signaled a waiter who brought him another drink from the refrigerator behind the bar.

Robert had been watching and, on seeing that David was obviously upset, came over. "Everything okay?"

"Yes, Robert, everything's fine. We … we'll be done here shortly. After that I want, no, I need you. If you'll just wait a bit more we'll go home."

Robert gave Simon a nasty look and returned to the bar. David took out the photographs and looked at them again.

"Any bite marks?"

"It was difficult to tell but, no."

"Then that only leaves one way for fluid to leave the body. We sometimes take nourishment that way, but only as an appetizer, not a full meal. Which, by the way, is a pint. Two if we're really hungry. And I can't think of any creature either human, animal, or natural monster like my kind who could do this sort of damage. Whatever this is, it's unearthly."

"I was afraid you'd say that. One more favor, if I may. I'm sure that you and your kin have some sort of social media group. Ask around if you will."

"Not to be coarse, Simon, but what's in it for me, or rather, us?"

"Favors owed, protection if needed, and no angry mobs with pitchforks and torches."

David laughed, Simon joined in as his friend said, "Wrong movie, but I get the idea. Now, it's time I left with Robert and left you with the bill. AB negative does not come cheap."

Simon Tombs sat on his balcony staring across the street at the sky above the Starry Night Hotel, a prestige hotel whose guests paid three to four times the average nightly stay for "personalized service." That meant breakfast in bed, 24-hour concierge service, and guaranteed tickets to all sporting events, plays, and musicals currently in Baltimore, at ticket price and a small handling fee, of course.

Simon usually enjoyed the view above the hotel, how the taller buildings on either side framed the starry blackness between them. He once mentioned to Fel that he felt as if he could see all the way to Heaven through that blackness. She laughed and told him that they *were* in Heaven, that this world, the universe it was in, and all the other universes that existed were all part of the Divine's domain.

Simon had rescued Fel from the Pit. He had taught her, cared for her, and, he liked to think, reformed and saved her. She was his lover and guardian demon who in the end saved him then flew away on new wings into another story. Now, as he looked above the Starry Night, all he could do was think of her and cherish the ache in his heart that was his love for her.

But not that night. That night he had locked his heart away as his mind worked on the problem before him.

He wasn't worried about finding the woman. Caitlin and her crew would canvass and watch the surveillance videos and eventually locate her. Simon's task was to discover her nature, discern her abilities, and figure out how to counter them.

He knew what she did and how she did it. Why was the question. Was she like David, a not yet known natural monster? If so, maybe she had to kill to survive. Or was she, as David had said, unearthly and killed in this manner because she enjoyed it, because it gave her pleasure far beyond what her victims felt in their last minutes.

With the sun coming up, Simon again read the reports, looked at the photos of the victims and crime scenes and thought about what he and David had discussed and what Caitlin had told him.

Something teased his mind, something that she said. No, he realized, it was something he had said, something about a ghost giving men pleasurable and painful dreams. "Ghost" had been a euphemism. People are inclined to believe in ghosts. They are less likely to believe in a succubus.

That might be it, he thought. *Instead of taking their essence in their dreams, she's escaped the Pit and is reveling in draining them dry in an act that not only kills them but might damn them as well.*

Where did she come from? No, I know where she came from, I just wonder how.

Some months ago

Everything was prepared. After a year of research and study, Brady Richmond was ready. He rented a storage unit, which gave him a large, open space. The circle he drew was geometrically perfect, as was the pentagram within it. Candles burned at the star's five points; its triangles inscribed with summoning runes. A cup of his blood lay at the precise center of the central pentagon. Wearing his freshly laundered robe, he began the ritual, speaking the words clearly, pronouncing them correctly.

"I command thee, demons of the Pit, to send one of your multitude to serve me. I give my blood as an offering. I would have a female, one of great beauty, trained in the arts of lust and desire, one who will obey my every command and satisfy my every need. Send her now, I command it."

His heart beating, his excitement growing, Brady waited in anticipation. He would spend a week doing all those things he had read about but had never done in real life. Once he was sated, he'd rest and do them all over again. Only then would he send his demon on a mission of vengeance to destroy, no, not destroy but to disfigure the women who had rejected him and the men who had bullied and mocked him.

Sex and vengeance. The thought came unbidden to his mind, but yes, that was what he wanted. In his heart, mind, and soul, that was what he wanted.

A minute went by. Then two, then five. Was there smoke forming? Was the level of blood diminishing?

The ritual should have worked, he thought. *Maybe I should repeat it? Repeat it twice. There's power in three.*

"That won't be necessary." The voice came from behind. "I heard you the first time."

Brady turned, and there she was. She was tall, her hair was long and red, her eyes green. She was dressed in a sheer white gown through which he could almost make out her firm breasts, her narrow waist, and the crimson shadow that hid the treasure between her legs.

"Am I everything you imagined?" Her voice was kind and gentle, more comforting than sensuous. "Yes, I see that I am."

Brady was naked beneath his robe and his excitement was evident. As she slowly walked toward him he backed up, matching her step by step, unknowingly crossing into the pentagram. Soon he was in its center, the back of his left foot upending the cup and spilling its contents.

"Perfect. Now lie down." Obeying, he lay in his blood. "Pull up your robe. Show yourself to me." When he did as she commanded she raised her gown and showed herself to him.

Brady almost lost it but controlled his passion long enough for the demon to mount him and take him inside her.

So good, so ... cold, he thought as he experienced the most intense pleasure he had ever had. He climaxed over and over, each spurt draining him of his life's energy. Finally, as his body convulsed in one last spasm, Brady Richmond noted how much the demon reminded him of his mother.

The demon stood. Looking down at the shriveled husk of her victim she laughed and said, "Was it as good for you as it was for me?" Then she was gone from the basement and loose upon the world.

Traffic noise woke Simon up. *I fell asleep*, he said to himself as soon as he was able to think. *And now I'm stiff in all the wrong places. What was I thinking of? Oh yeah, how the succubus had escaped the Pit. It's not impossible, Fel did. Probably a summoning, some unprepared idiot who thought he'd get his heart's desires by bringing forth a demon. He was probably her first victim and if he lived alone, his body won't be found until his lease is up, his house loan called in, or his home sold for non-payment of taxes. In the end, the how and why don't matter, it's the where.*

Again he thought of Fel, and how she might have been able to find this demon. And thinking of how well they had worked together made him miss her even more.

David called him.

"You owe me, Simon. And not just a glass or two of the rich, red stuff. After our meeting, I did as you asked and reached out to my kin. Most were, let's say, reluctant. The general opinion was it was not our circus so you mortals could clean up after the elephants. But I mentioned how easily we could be blamed and how humans tend to destroy that which they fear. I evoked the image of angry villagers with pitchforks and torches and that did it. Frederick, they lead the kin in Frederick County, among ourselves we go by the name of our territory, told me about a storage facility in New Market. The renter of one of its units hadn't paid his bill. The other day the manager opened it up and found a dried-up corpse and occult paraphernalia. Frederick has a lot of influence in their territory so it was put down to an accident with only a small news article in the local paper."

"Were photographs taken?"

"Better than that. Frederick had the unit locked down. They'll meet you, and only you, there tonight."

New Market is less than an hour away from Baltimore. Simon arrived at the facility slightly before nine. He was met by a small, thin person wearing a dark grey sweat suit. Their hair was cut close and their hands showed signs of having done rough work in the past.

"Good evening," Frederick said. Their voice bore the harshness of a heavy smoker. *Pre-change*, Simon thought. He knew better than to ask. One did not talk to vampires about their lives "before."

"Thank you for this," he said.

"Thank you for coming, Mr. Tombs. Or rather, Simon, if I may?" Simon nodded. "Baltimore was very convincing that what affects some affects all. We had the husk plague here in this county and it looked iffy. Let's just say that the stakes were high and figuratively sharpened. That's when I knew I had to take a more active interest in my territory. Thank the Divine that there are more than a few kinky people running things. Some digital photos of them having their necks and other things sucked was all it took. But you're here to see this," Frederick said, opening the unit's passage door.

No sooner was Simon inside that the smell of dark magic hit him. It was at least two months old but was still strong, its stench hanging in the air. He knew a spell that would dissipate it. He'd use it before he left.

The pentagram was large, covering half the floor. Simon studied it as he walked around.

"What do you think?" Frederick asked from the doorway.

"You're not coming in?" Frederick shook their head. *How do I put this?* Simon asked himself before deciding *What the hell.* "Do you need an invitation?"

Frederick smiled. "No, but thank you for asking. There are not many who realize that some of the old ways still bind us. But the manager of the facility gave me the keys, which was invitation enough. I just do not wish to enter. No offense, Simon, but I want nothing to do with magic, especially this kind."

"Good choice, unlike what we have here. Whoever drew this did not know what they were doing. It's too elaborate, too chaotic. One needs order to command the chaos of the Pit. It is, however, enough to attract the attention of something down below and give it access. But not enough to control it. What was the fool's name?"

"The dead man was Brady Richmond. I had county PD look into him. No wife, no family, a few friends, none of whom mourned him. We burned his body after a friendly doctor listed 'natural causes' as the cause of death."

"Unnatural causes would be more accurate, but one can't put that on a death certificate."

"No, one can't. Just wondering, could you use what Richmond drew to summon the demon back to it."

Simon thought for a moment. "Possibly, if it was drawn properly and specifically for her. I'd more likely call up something else, and that's not a problem we need right now. Would you like me to get rid of it for you?"

"If you would. Are you sure you won't need it?"

Simon closed his eyes and opened his mind, concentrating on the feeling of evil pervading the unit. There were several kinds. Richmond's for planning the summons and opening the way. His intent for the demon. The manner of his death. The pentagram itself. And finally the demon. There was something alluring about its evil, no, *her* evil, for it was definitely female.

I would know you anywhere, Simon thought, *no matter in what form Richmond bound you.*

Simon opened his eyes. "I'm very sure. Better step back."

Standing in the doorway, Simon spoke his spell.

Cool night air rushed into the unit, displacing the miasma of evil. Clouds formed at the ceiling and rain fell on the floor. The pentagram and the symbols it contained hissed, then smoked, then slowly sank into the floor until it was gone.

"Where did it go?" Frederick asked.

"To Hell, where one day it might prove useful."

Simon closed the door. "Tell the manager to have this professionally cleaned. By crime scene clean-up people if possible. They know how to clean. Make sure to tell them to treat the unit as a biohazard."

"I will do that. I'll even have a priest there to bless the cleaning equipment."

"Good idea. And now, Frederick, I'd best head back. There's still a succubus to catch. Thank you for your help."

"And thank you. You know, Simon, you're as attractive as Baltimore said you were. And I *would* like a taste." Simon prepared himself for the request. It would not be his first time. "But, no offense, I do not think I want what's in you inside of me."

"No offense taken, Frederick. And as enjoyable as it might have been, I think you choose wisely."

Charm had found something. This time he and Simon met at the Perry Hall Diner . Once their coffee, sweet tea, and potato skins arrived, Simon asked,

"Caitlin's not coming?"

Charm shook his head. "Nah, the major's got Lieutenant Rankin watching her. Neither one can figure out how she's doing it."

"Doing what?"

"Tombs, when the sarge came back, to make up her squad they gave her the detectives with the lowest clearance rates. And yeah, I was one of them. They were hoping that her part of the murder board would bleed red with unclosed cases. A good excuse to send us back to patrol and her someplace like Cold Case."

"But you fooled them."

"We did," Charm said with some pride. "Thanks to her. She's got this knack of telling who's guilty and by how much. So right now we've got as much black on the board as anyone."

"And why is this bad?"

"Like I said, they don't know how she's doing it and it bothers the hell out of them. They think she's pulling a fiddle and they'd love to catch her doing something like, well, hanging with you. Why are you smiling like that?"

"Confusion to our enemies, Charm. No one messes with my friends, which include Caitlin, you, and the rest of your pack."

"You calling us dogs?"

"Police dogs. Now then, why this meeting?"

"I think we got her, Tombs."

"Tell me a story, Charm. Once upon a time …"

"The sarge was right, you're a weird dude. I took Marks's driver's license photo around the Inner Harbor and Harbor East bars where the conventioneers go. You know, the single guys and the ones who think their marriage licenses only apply in the state where they live. I crapped out so I tried Federal Hill. Ever hear of a place called Humpty's?"

"Heard of it but I've never been there. Is it a good place to get lucky?"

Charm caught his meaning and smiled. "In more ways than one, I'm told. And I got lucky in the way my wife Molly won't mind. A waiter named Brian recognized the photo.

"'Yes,' he said. 'He was in here a few days ago. Left here with a sometime pro. She's a tall, slender redhead with nice boobs and no bra. She looks like she could be anybody you want her to be. Goes by the name Brady.'"

Simon was visibly excited. "What was that name?"

"Brady. Why, you know her?"

"Finish your story, Then I'll tell mine."

"According to Brian, this Brady comes in every few weeks. Now that got me as excited as her name got you. So I showed the photos of the other two vics. Care to guess?"

"They each left with Brady."

"Got it in one. Now tell me your story."

Simon told Charm about the demonic summoning in New Market that let a succubus loose on the world, or at least Baltimore. "The damned fool who set her free was named Brady Richmond."

"Damn. The bitch took his name. You know what we have to do now?" Charm answered his own question. "Stake out Humpty's and wait for a tall redhead to walk in."

"I'll leave that to you. Meanwhile, I'll set the trap."

It was later that evening. Simon was asleep, dreaming of angels in flight. There were two of them. One was blond and bright, her eyes blue, her youthful face a mix of hope and determination. She carried a flaming sword. The other angel was dark and dangerous, her gray wings singed black at their tips. Her sword was more substantial but no less deadly.

They danced in the air, their flight paths interweaving, coming closer and closer with each pass. Collision seemed imminent but then they stopped, turned, and looked down on Simon. Smiling, they dove toward him and …

BAM! BAM! BAM!

The noise woke Simon from the dream. As the angels left him, it repeated,

BAM! BAM! BAM!

He knew it for what it was, a police knock. Three to five blows, made with the pinky side of a closed fist. It was loud and insistent.

No cry of "Open up." No threats of forceful entry. No swinging ram smashing open the door. This was not *the police*. Fully awake now, he realized it was a police officer with access. And there was only one of them. An angel in her own right, albeit a mortal one.

"Just a minute, Caitlin," Simon called out then thought, *Door, open.* He felt her enter. "Start the coffee while I get dressed. Unless you rather I didn't?"

No reply. Caitlin usually had some answers to his joking propositions but tonight, nothing. He dressed and found Caitlin sitting at his kitchen table. The coffee was brewing. Caitlin had found the chocolate chip cookies.

"You talked to Charm."

She nodded. "I haven't told him too much about what you can do. Hell, I'm not even sure myself. So I thought I'd come to ask you myself. We know what she is and where she's from. We've got fluids from the victims that aren't theirs. So why can't you track her through that magic you did to find that Ripper thing?"

The coffee was ready. Simon poured two cups and sat beside her. Munching on a cookie, he said between bites,

"This Brady …"

"Call it a monster," Caitlin said angrily. "Call it a thing or a demon, but don't give her a human name. Especially one she stole."

"Okay," Simon said quietly. Knowing Caitlin, he suspected that she had been pulling more than double shifts, running her squad, looking for the demon, and shorting herself of sleep. Now that they had a lead, and a damn good one, she wanted it done and over. She wanted to kill this thing and throw its dead body on the desk of Lieutenant Rankin.

She's not thought through the endgame, he told himself. *No matter, I'm working on that. Carefully written false reports that the Brass will have no choice but to accept. As the man in the movie said, "They can't handle the truth."*

"I thought of that. But making that kind of contact with a demon is much like summoning it. It could follow the line back to me, to us, rather, since you'd probably insist on being there. I do not need an angry demon coming after me, especially since I just finished putting this place back together. I have a plan but you'll have to be patient. Trust me."

"Never thought I'd say it but, I do. I just hate to wait. I'd better be going."

"You okay to drive home? I have a spare bedroom with a door that locks from the inside."

"Her bedroom. That last time, Fel and me ... No, Barbara's waiting downstairs. I told her if she didn't hear from me in an hour she should break in, shoot you, and we'd write it up as justifiable. So like I said, I should leave."

"Simon, why are you phoning me so early? It's almost dawn."
"I have a quick question. Where do you buy your bedsheets?"

Simon, Caitlin, and Charm met at the White Marsh Diner for a council of war.

"Surveillance of Humpty's is approved and set," Caitlin said.

"How did you get, who is it, Ranklin, to approve?"

"I told him that we had a lead on the person who's been spreading the current version of the husk. 'Patient Zero,' I called her. I said she was a tall redhead who had some kind of natural immunity, that she hated men and so was transmitting it sexually."

"And he bought this?"

"He's an idiot, Simon. All he was thinking about was how to grab the credit to push himself up a couple of notches on the promotional list. That and the very convincing medical documentation Terry put together out of whole cloth."

"Well done, Charm. I'm impressed."

"Be impressed with my wife, Tombs. She's a wizard at that sort of thing and an angel for doing it without asking too many questions."

"Give her my thanks. Caitlin, Charm, the rooms are reserved and the preparations are in place. Based on her previous feedings, she could make her appearance at any time. So I suppose it's time for me to become a regular at Humpty's."

"Why you?" challenged Charm.

"Why not me?" Simon argued. "I've faced creatures like this

before. I've got the tools and weapons to use against her. If things go bad before I can get her into the room, well, it won't be pretty but it will be over."

"Why not you? Let me tell you. You're not a cop. I don't know exactly what you are but you're not a cop. You may have been invited but it's not your party. It's ours. Our case, our suspect, our responsibility. And besides, look at you. You don't look like you've ever paid for it in your life. If you have, it was in some kind of a fancy house where the women cost more than I make in a month, counting overtime. Me, well, to be honest, I've never paid for it either, but I look like I might."

Simon was about to object but Charm went on. "One more thing. I can't sense it, being a mere human and all, but I'm willing to bet that whatever this creature is will feel your magic as soon as she walks into Humpty's. If she does, she's out of there and we get to start all over. Assuming she doesn't leave the city and start somewhere else."

Simon thought about what Charm said for a moment. He turned to Caitlin and asked, "Is this what you think?"

"I think Terry's right. It's a risk and I'd rather see you taking it, but he's right."

"Thanks, Sarge, but I figure as long as I keep my dick in my pants I'll be safe."

"One more thing, Charm, and forgive me for asking, but how does your wife feel about this?"

Charm scowled and looked as if he was going to tell Simon to go to the Hell the demon had come from. But he shrugged it off and said, "What she doesn't know and all that. But what she does know is the score, that I might make it to retirement but there's a chance I won't. That every day I go to work might be the day I don't come back."

Simon nodded. The Question had been asked. All that was left was to respect the Choice made by a brave man.

"Very well, Charm. You be the bait and bring her to the trap. Just remember your lines and she'll be one dead rodent. Now then, this is a relatively new place. Let's test the kitchen. Dinner's on me."

The original Hotel Royale had been built in the latter part of the nineteenth century, back when the Howard Street corridor was the heart of Baltimore's shopping and entertainment district. It declined along with the rest of the "downtown" businesses. It wasn't until the Inner Harbor and Harbor East became the new heart of Baltimore's tourist trade that the Royale's owners, who had Outfit ties from back before Capone got his first scar, decided to move the hotel there.

The current Hotel Royale is located on the southeast corner of Eastern Avenue and President Street. It has the old-world charm of the previous one along with all-new technology, and a speakeasy-style casino on the top floor. To enter you need "the password," which is easily obtained from the concierge. (It's usually but not always "swordfish.")

Simon was not interested in gambling. Nor did he care to drink a Pepper Special on the casino's balcony with its view of the Inner Harbor. No, he was in his ninth-floor room, waiting for the rat to take the cheese and thinking of all the things that might go wrong.

It was the fourth night of the stakeout. Caitlin and Charm had started it two weeks after Eddie Marks died. Charm was on the inside, waiting for a tall, slender redhead to walk in.

"What if it goes for someone other than Terry?" Caitlin had asked Simon.

"Not likely," he replied. "Demons, succubi and incubi especially, respond to desire. Satan designed them for it. Better to tempt weak humans into sin. So a demon such as Brady would respond to the one who desired it the most. And I'd bet a great deal of money that no one in Humpty's wants Brady more than Charm."

"Let's hope you're right. But in case you're wrong, me and

volunteers from my squad will be outside the bar, ready to take action if things turn sideways or if you're wrong and the demon leaves with someone else."

"What kind of action?"

"Whatever it takes, Simon, up to and including lethal force. I won't have this bitch hunting humans in my city. So if we have to, we'll kill her and take the fall if we have to."

No, you won't, Simon thought. *No one in the city government, especially those in the secretive Third Branch, want the citizens of Baltimore to know that there are monsters among them.*

He handed Caitlin a metal box. "In that case, you'll need this."

"What's in it?"

"Several clips of .40 caliber cartridges for your pistols. They've been blessed by the regional representative of the Vatican's Holy Office and will stop a demon. However, the effects are quite dramatic — loud noises, hellfire, and the screams of the damned. So tell your detectives to use them only as a last resort."

And that's only some of the things that can go wrong, Simon thought as he again reviewed the plans he and Charm had made.

Opening the connecting door between his room and the next, he stood in the double doorway and inspected the room Charm was to use.

I hope this works, he thought. Certain that he had done everything he could, he reminded himself that magic was largely a matter of intent. That damned fool Richmond had intended to summon a demon. Despite doing everything wrong, he did. Now Simon intended to destroy that demon and hoped he had done everything right.

Time will tell, he thought, closing the connecting door and looking to see what was on television.

He was halfway through an episode of a TV mystery where a bumbling detective made all the wrong deductions yet somehow managed to expose the killer when his text alert buzzed.

<rat has the cheese. ready the trap.>

Simon silently thanked several deities and the Universe itself.

He turned off the TV and closed his eyes. Picturing the other room in his mind, he said a few activating words.

Simon, Charm, and Caitlin had timed how long it took to get from Humpty's to the Royale. Simon checked his watch; they should be near.

Calm down, Simon, he thought. *Go to your happy place.* Then he realized he was already there — on the edge, anticipating action, waiting for it to begin, ready for the upcoming battle. Simon savored this moment because once things got started, he'd have no time to think, only to do and hopefully not die.

Then he heard it, a key in the lock of the adjoining room. The sound of the door opening.

"What a nice room. Do you come here often?"

A woman's voice, sultry and seductive. Despite not having seen her, Simon found himself getting excited from that one brief sentence. *Stay strong, Charm*, he thought.

"Well, I haven't come yet."

Brady laughed at Charm's poor joke as if it was the funniest one she'd ever heard.

"Let's see what we can do to fix that. No, how do you want me?"

Stick to the script.

"Um, it's like this." As they had rehearsed, and wasn't that awkward for all, Charm managed to sound eager and embarrassed at the same time. "I mean, I love my wife, but she can be demanding at times, especially in bed. We always do it the way she wants. I mean, even when I'm on top, she's still in control. Do you know what I mean?"

Is she close to him? Is she kissing him?

"No, not yet. I want you in bed, naked and under the covers. Then I'll undress while you watch. When I get in with you, you just lie there while I do, well, whatever I want to you. But, er, don't worry, I won't take long."

"Don't worry about that. I promise you you'll last longer than you ever have. It will be as good for me as it is for you."

Wishing he could see what was going on, Simon pictured the demon waking toward the bed, shedding her clothes, getting under the …

The screaming started. Simon rushed through the unlocked connecting door. He saw Charm backing away, his pistol in his hand. He looked toward the bed. The redhead was writhing and burning under bedsheets made from soil taken from a saint's consecrated grave and mixed with holy water and some strands of angel's hair that Nika had left on his pillow. The sheet the demon was lying on was similarly made. She was trapped, her body burning on both sides.

Her screams were loud, piercing, and painful. The stench of burning demon flesh was terrible. *Good thing I disabled the smoke alarms*, Simon thought.

The demon tried to escape, tried to get out of bed, but to no avail. The binding sigils he had inscribed on the mattress held her in place.

Unwilling to see even a creature as evil as she was suffer so badly, Simon was about to say the words that would send its damned soul back to the Pit when she turned and saw him.

"You!" she shouted; the whole of her hatred contained in that one word. "I know you. We all know you," she yelled. "You stole souls from us. You and that bitch you saved beat back our hordes. Damn you, Simon Tombs."

Enduring pain worse than it had suffered in Hell, the demon somehow rose from the bed. Arms outstretched, she rushed at Simon, hands up and talons extended, ready to savage him and drag him to Hell with her.

Simon backed away, drawing a knife fashioned to rip demon flesh and hoping it would be enough. He never found out.

There was the sound of a gunshot. In the confines of the small room, it seemed louder than any of the screaming the demon had done. The blessed bullet that entered the demon's back was everything Simon had promised Caitlin it would be.

The demon ignited in a hellfire flame that was confined only to her. From her mouth came a banshee scream that ran through the hotel, waking the just and frightening some of the guilty into repentance.

Tearing his gaze from the demon's burning body, Simon looked over at Charm. The detective was pale and his hands, still holding his pistol, were shaking. But there was excitement in his eyes and a smile on his face from doing a needed job well done.

"Damn, Tombs," Charm said as he holstered his weapon. "I have to party with you more often."

Charm took a moment as his adrenaline rush and the thrill of battle left him. Pointing toward what was left of the body he asked, "What about that thing? Gonna be hard to explain a shot, burned up corpse."

"A worry for tomorrow, Charm. For now, let's put the hotel sheets back on the bed. The ones I brought need to be burned."

Dog Eat Dog

Douglas Serrano grew up in the family business. That business was crime, his father being a cousin to the local director of the Outfit.

There was no question as to what Douglas would do when he finished college. His father Robert, aka Big Bobby, had made it clear that Douglas would be going to college.

"Why college, Pops?" Douglas had objected. "Uncle Vince said I could start right after high school."

"Cousin Vincent said that you *could* start after high school. But he said it was up to me and not you. And I say it's after college. And that's that. The first thing you learn in this life is that you listen and obey. If you can't do that, you won't be in this life anymore. Got it?"

Douglas got it, including the implicit threat. There's the Life and your life, and a guy could lose both by not following the rules.

"May I ask why college?"

"You may."

It took Douglas a few beats before he realized that Big Bobby was not going to answer. It took him a few more to work out why. He had not asked the question; he had only asked if he could. And so, "Why college?"

Big Bobby smiled. "Because, Dougie, it's a dog-eat-dog world out there, and if you're going to get ahead, you got to be tougher and smarter than all the other dogs. You already have smarts; college will teach you how to use them. As for tough, your uncles already have a few summer jobs lined up for you."

"Like what, internships or something."

"Something like that, only you'll get paid. And you'll learn things college doesn't teach you."

Douglas did his four years, graduating, to his family's

amusement, with a degree in criminal justice. As Big Bobby promised, he spent his summers learning about the Outfit from the inside. He ran book, he made loans, he boosted trucks, and he worked with the high-end B&E gangs. He did everything his "uncles" asked of him and proved to be good at all of them.

There was, however, one thing that he had never been asked to do. When Douglas was a junior in high school, his Uncle Max took him out to the country and taught Douglas how to shoot — at a distance with long arms and closer in with pistols and revolvers.

"You got the eye, Dougie," Max told him after Dougie not only showed he could hit his target but the parts of the target Max told him to hit. "Just one more thing and I'll take you to your Aunt Sally's house where she'll have one of her girls teach you other things you need to know. See that mannequin over there?" When Douglas nodded, Max handed him a .32 hammerless Smith and Wesson. "Take this and stick it in your belt. It's loaded so be careful it don't go off. If it does, there'll be no reason to take you to Sally's. Now, I want you to walk over to the dummy, pull your piece, put two in its head, then drop the piece. After you do, just walk away casual-like. Always walk, never run."

Douglas was not a fool. He knew what this was a rehearsal for. Still, he was only seventeen and half his mind was on what Aunt Sally's girl might teach him. He couldn't help but give his uncle a look.

"Yeah, kid, I know and you may never be asked. But you gotta be ready. A big part of our life is death. It's like your dad says, 'It's a dog-eat-dog world,' and sometimes dogs that go bad have to be put down. Get me?"

Douglas got it. Without a word, he broke open the .32 and checked the load. Then he snapped it shut, walked over to the dummy, put two in its head, and dropped the piece.

"Good job, kid. Now, about Sally's, you want a young one or an old one?"

It was two months after graduation. Douglas was on a crew that was selling stolen designer jeans to small clothing stores that otherwise couldn't afford them. When he got back to his apartment Big Bobby was waiting. "What's up, Pops?"

"Pulling you off the crew for now, Dougie. We need you to go to Wildwood. There's a guy there, he runs our carny booths on the Boardwalk. He's been skimming our take."

"Don't they all, Pops?"

"But he's skimming too deep. He needs taking care of."

Douglas did not need to be told how. All he said was, "Uncle Max out at the farm that time."

"Yeah, it's time you got blooded. It's all been set up. Here's your contact." Big Bobby handed his son a slip of paper. "Take your time and do it right."

Something clicked in Douglas's head. "About the contact. Whoever it is, call and cancel. What's the mark's name?"

"Shelly, Shelly Green. Short for Sheldon. Guys call him Shecky. Why?"

"Call him. Tell him there's an out-of-town problem and set up a meet. Some place quiet and private. The less people who know the better."

Big Bobby thought for a moment. "Good idea. Say, Dougie, you okay with this?"

Douglas knew that this was his way out. All he had to say was no and he'd be off the job. But he didn't want to be on a crew all his life. A loser selling clothes to other losers.

"Like you say, Pops, it's a dog-eat-dog world. I'll bring you back some taffy."

"Make it fudge. Taffy's bad for my fillings."

Four days later, shortly after sunrise, the body of Shelly Green, aka Shecky, was found face down on the beach a few blocks south of the Boardwalk, a .38 Smith and Wesson next to his right hand. Despite the fact that he'd been shot in the back of the head, the police ruled it a suicide.

The job was done so cleanly that Douglas Serrano was called on to do more of them. He accepted them all, each time with a shrug and an "It's a dog-eat-dog world." Soon he became known as Dog. "Do this or we'll sic the Dog on you," became a common threat.

At first, Dog just did Outfit-related hits — cheats, traitors, those that strayed from the pack or threatened to go to the cops or the feds. But then innocents became involved — family members and friends the target may have talked to, witnesses who were in the wrong place at the wrong time and thought it their civic duty to go to the police, union workers who insisted on honest representation, and shop owners chosen as an example to others.

It was killing these that began to bother him. Those who, like him, were in the Life knew that death could be their end. But the others, he began to feel for them, knowing even as he pulled the trigger that what he was doing was wrong, even by his standards. But he was in too deep. Any refusal would put him outside the pack. So for another ten years, Dog practiced his chosen profession, killing people at the command of his masters.

Then Dog got orders that a man named Joe Ballard had to die. He didn't ask why. At that point, he no longer cared. He'd do the job then maybe hit a place like Sally's for some quick release before going home to drink enough so he'd sleep without dreaming.

Dog followed Ballard for three days before he decided where he'd do the job. Every day after leaving work, Ballard would cut down an alley to the next street to catch the bus home.

Easy job, Dog thought. *Walk up to him, put two in his head, drop the gun, and walk away.*

And that's how it went, or should have gone. The first bullet went into Ballard's head and stayed. But he fell too fast, and so the second missed and struck and killed a woman named Annette McKay. Annette was a wife, the mother of a young boy, and worst of all for Dog, the niece of the city's Archbishop.

"Someone's got to pay for this one, Dougie."

This from Carney Duncan, the man who had taken Uncle

Vincent's place in the Outfit. Duncan's use of "Dougie" instead of Dog left no doubt who that "someone" had to be. He got sloppy and screwed up and now he had to pay. In a way, it was a relief. The drink no longer stopped the dreams.

"I'll do it myself. I'll leave a note confessing the kills. Ballard's, the girl's, and any others you want to add."

"They want more than that, Dougie. The word is that they want the whole show — arrest, perp walk, show trial, and execution."

"You've got it set up already, haven't you?"

Duncan nodded. "A couple of tame dicks are waiting outside." *So that's why we met in a hotel bar instead of Duncan's office,* Dog thought just as Duncan asked, "What I want to know is if we can count on you? After all, it's a big difference between sitting on death row waiting to ride the lightning and being thrown into the general population where a dog becomes everybody's bitch."

"Well, Carney, when you put it that way, I guess you can count on me."

Dog was indicted and soon the day of his trial came. Everyone was assembled and everything fixed. It was meant to be a show trial that would sell papers for a week and propel the judge, the District Attorney, and the ever-so-cooperative public defender to higher office. Two civilian witnesses, who had not been anywhere near the shooting, were prepared to testify that yes, they had seen the shooter and yes, that was him sitting at the defense table. The lab guys would confirm that Dog's prints were on the recovered weapon (Dog had worn gloves) and the gun matched the recovered bullets (which had been smashed beyond recognition). The presiding judge was not one to show mercy and seemed to enjoy sentencing men, and the occasional woman, to death.

The show was ready but Dog decided not to play.

When the judge asked, "How does the defendant plead?" Dog quietly answered,

"Guilty, Your Honor."

This was not how things were supposed to go. No trial meant no publicity and no names or stories in the paper.

"Are you sure, Mr. Sorenson?"

"Yes, Your Honor

"Would you like to consult with your attorney?"

"No, Your Honor."

"Then based on your plea, I find you guilty of two counts of first-degree murder. And I sentence you to be executed at a time and by a method determined by the state."

Dog was taken to the state penitentiary and placed in a single cell on Death Row where he had plenty of time to think as he awaited execution. He thought about the choices he had made in his life, and of his mistakes. He finally decided that they were mostly one and the same. He did not bother blaming others — his father, his "uncles," the ones who selected his targets and the ones who set them up and pointed them out. He could have said "no" to the Life. He could have said "no" when told to kill Green. Each time he took a job and picked up a gun he could have said "no" and put it down. He never asked why these people had to die. He just shrugged and said, "It's a dog-eat-dog world." Alone in his cell with too much time to think, Dog found that that explanation no longer cut it. Nor did the rationalization of "They were already dead. If I didn't pull the trigger someone else would."

Father Louis Damien was the penitentiary chaplain who ministered to those on Death Row. He listened, he consoled, he prayed with the men and heard their confessions. On one of his visits, Dog talked to Father Louis about his mistakes, his choices, and what he'd been thinking.

"Do you regret your actions, Douglas?"

"Maybe, Father, I don't know. Maybe if I knew why they died I could say. The guilty ones, the ones in the Life, probably not. The ones outside the Life, the civilians who didn't ask to be a part of it, the Annette McKays and the ones like her — yeah, those I regret."

"Does it matter if they were in or out of what you call 'the Life?' You took from them the most precious thing of all."

"Their lives?"

"The chance that you've been given. To repent their sins and make their peace with God."

Dog didn't reply to that. When Father Louis saw that he wasn't going to, he said, "Think about it, Douglas," and left to minister to another of the condemned.

A few days later Father Louis again visited Dog.

"You're coming more often, Father. Time must be running out."

"It runs out for everyone, Douglas, just sooner for some."

"Yeah, I get it. Listen, I've been thinking about what you said, how I robbed these people of their last chance. And how some of these people, hell, probably a lot of them, didn't deserve what they got."

"And what did you decide?"

"How does this confession stuff work?"

"Through me, you tell God that you're truly sorry for your sins and ask, no, in your case beg His Forgiveness. Then I absolve you of your sins."

"And that's it, my slate is wiped clean."

"No, there's usually penance."

"Makes sense. You have to pay for your sins. No free ride except the one I'm taking on the lightning. Do you think that will do it?"

"That's between you and God, Douglas. Shall we begin?"

Father Louis returned three days later, accompanied by the warden and two guards.

"I guess it's time," Dog said to the priest.

"Yes, it is."

"I've been thinking it over. Whatever the price, I'm willing to pay it."

That was the last thing Dog said before he was strapped into the wooden chair and the lightning ran through his body, sending him from this world to the next.

⚱

Dog woke up in the woods. There were trees, what sounded like birds, and the rustling of animals in the bushes. He stood and looked around and, like Adam, realized he was naked.

"Is this Heaven?" he asked out loud, for some reason expecting an answer. None came. Given the circumstances, he wondered if this was Eden and, if so, would there be an Eve to share it with him.

More than I deserve, he thought and decided to explore. Before he could take more than a few steps, he heard growling.

He turned and there behind him was a gigantic hound. It looked more like a Rottweiler than anything, albeit with a touch of Doberman. It was larger than a car and, except for its red eyes and sharp white teeth, was black. No, not black. Black is a color, this beast, this … dog, was a shadow come to life.

This is not Heaven, Dog (the man) said to himself. *This is payment for my sins.*

For a minute, man and dog simply stared at each other, the dog's growl soft and menacing. Then the dog locked eyes with him, putting one foot in front of the other as it stalked its prey.

It was a race he could not win but still Dog ran, somehow knowing what was going to happen when the shadow beast caught him.

Dog eats Dog, he thought as he ran into then stumbled through the woods. *Fair enough.*

The Book of Flambeau

The Basilica of the Assumption of Mary is located in the heart of Baltimore. Some would say, as it was the first cathedral built in the newly formed United States, that it was also at the heart of the Catholic Church in America.

Simon Tombs would not disagree. Each time he entered the basilica he felt its majesty and the power that had grown from the belief and faith of centuries of worshippers. One could draw from that, he often thought, if one dared.

Simon had last attended services in the basilica on Christmas – the midnight mass. He was accompanied by the angel Nika whom he had helped find the new Spirit of the Season. After mass, they went to Sebastian's where he introduced her to hotter chocolate and something Murphy the bartender called a "Twisted Elf." She stayed with him until New Year's Eve, then disappeared like a heavenly Cinderella when the countdown hit zero. The memory of her last kiss lingered long after he realized he was dancing alone.

There had been no one since. Oh, he'd had his chances, but after a demon then an angel what else was there? He looked forward to finding out.

On the day in question, Simon sat in the fourth pew from left center. He was not there to worship, or to reminiscence. No, he had been summoned by the highest authority in Baltimore. Maybe "summoned" was the wrong word. It was more a request based on friendship, favors done, and secrets shared.

While he waited, he thought back to that last mass. The priest had given a good sermon, contrasting the "presents" that were to be received that day with the "Presence" of the Divine and how "His Presence was the present that God had given the world."

"You know," Nika said much later that morning in Simon's

apartment, "he was good. And almost got it right."

Simon would have asked about the "almost" but then Nika insisted on celebrating the joy of the season yet again.

His thoughts were interrupted by a priest emerging from the sacristy. He was a small man, no more than five-six, with thinning black hair and round black glasses. If he were a criminal, Simon thought, he'd probably be known as "Professor" or "the Owl" and would likely be very deadly.

"Mr. Tombs?" the priest asked in a gentle voice.

Simon stood and left his pew to greet him. "Yes. And you are Father Bozell?"

In what was obviously a much-repeated gesture, the priest used his forefinger to push his glasses tight against his face. "Not that it matters, but it's Monsignor Bozell, Henry Bozell."

"Monsignor, then," Simon held out his hand. The monsignor shook it. "I've always wondered, what's the difference? Are you one step above a priest and one below a bishop?"

Bozell chuckled. "There is no real difference. Just a title given as a reward for service." Another chuckle. "And a subtle hint that you're likely never to be appointed a bishop."

Simon smiled. "Well, if you ever want to move up, let me know. I have some friends in high places."

"Yes, I know, his Excellency."

"Oh, higher than that. I was once, no, make that twice investigated by the Vatican's Holy Office. I was cleared both times and made some close friends. Now then, the archbishop said you needed my help but didn't say why. "

Thrown a bit by Simon's last comment, Bozell pushed his glasses back and said, "Well, Mr. Tombs, I think I should show you."

Simon followed the monsignor to the second level of the church. A hallway behind the choir loft led to a solid oak door mounted in a steel frame and secured by a key and combination Manchester lock.

Protecting something important, Simon thought.

Bozell opened the door to reveal a sizable library then stepped aside to allow his guest to take it all in.

Simon wandered, looking at the books on the shelves, which is the only thing to do when entering a library for the first time. There were books with which he was very familiar and others he had only heard about. Some of the books were mere rumors and others were believed to have never existed.

Having completed his tour, Simon asked the monsignor, "Your middle name wouldn't be Lucien, would it?"

Bozell smiled at this reference to the Library of the Lord of Dreams. "Welcome to a branch of the Vatican's Secret Archives, Mr. Tombs. As you have no doubt noted, on these shelves you'll find books that have been deemed dangerous to one's mind, body, or soul, or to the world at large."

"And gospels that contradict accepted doctrine, or letters that reveal that some of the saints were not so holy, or other works that might be embarrassing to the Church."

"Well, yes," Bozell admitted.

"By the way, I have it on good authority that the Gospel of Judas is definitely a forgery."

Surprised, the monsignor did that thing he did with his glasses but before he could ask "On what authority," Simon went on.

"But let's talk about why I'm here. It's about that missing book, isn't it?"

"How did you … oh, the gap on the shelves."

"Yes, it's the only one. Based on the filing system you seem to be using, Alexandrian isn't it, it's something dangerous."

"Yes, it is, very. Please, have a seat."

They sat at a small, round table. It, its four hardback chairs, and an old laptop were the only furnishings in the room other than the bookshelves.

"The *Book of Flambeau*. Flambeau was a late 15th-century philosopher and reputed sorcerer. He was condemned about 1500 not for his beliefs but for his practices — unholy sacrifices, raising demons, murder, and rape. Had he lived in our times we would have regarded him as a serial killer. Such was his evil that not only was he burned at the stake, but the fire was kept burning for five days to ensure that his entire body was reduced to ash. The ashes and what parts of him failed to burn were then buried in a place known only to the gravedigger."

Bozell paused as if to collect his thoughts, then went on. "Flambeau kept a diary. It was this that the Inquisition used to condemn him. He also created a grimoire of the spells, chants, and procedures he used in his evil work. It was said to be very detailed and more specific than any such work before or after. This was not presented at his trial but rather taken directly to the secret archives."

"Why not just destroy it?"

"A half-century before, a similar work was burned. It took four holy scholars and one future saint two weeks to destroy all the demons that were released. As I said, it was taken to the archives where it remained until the Vatican decided not to, well, keep all its eggs in one basket. It and the other books within these walls were entrusted to me, and I have lost it."

"And I am here to help you get it back, Monsignor," Simon said with more confidence than he was feeling.

"I'm glad to hear that. Now, any immediate thoughts on our … problem? Like, how whoever it was got into the safe?"

Simon shook his head. "That's not a problem. Not to brag, but a man of my … abilities could have that door opened in, oh, two or three minutes." At the look on Bozell's face, Simon explained. "Doors have two functions, to protect and to allow entry and exit. Once one knows the trick, it's easy to convince a door to do one rather than the other. But there are more mundane ways as well. For instance, who has access to the passcode and key? Besides you, of course."

Simon gave the monsignor a look he had learned from Caitlin Hood, one that conveyed suspicion during the asking of an innocent question.

The somewhat flustered cleric pushed back his glasses, and

sputtered, "Only … me, the cathedral dean, and the archbishop. But you don't suspect …"

"Not you, Monsignor. If you had taken it, you would have simply closed the gap and it's likely the book's loss would never have been noticed. As for the other two, let's keep them on our list of suspects but down at the bottom."

The thought that either of the two men he held in high regard could be thieves or worse bothered Bozell. He looked at Simon, hoping the man was joking. No, while there was a smile on the man's face, he clearly was not ruling anyone out. He found himself wishing for a large brandy even as Simon said,

"Any determined thief could have gotten through the door. So the question is, who knew the Book of Flambeau was in your keeping?"

"Anyone who accessed the Vatican's website and searched for 'secret archives' or something similar."

It was Simon's turn to be amazed. Seeing his surprise made the cleric feel a little better. "It's all part of the pope's desire to be more transparent. Of course, we just list titles and authors, if the latter are known. And we don't provide samples or descriptions of the contents."

"So if I were to search for the unexpurgated version of *The Way of a Man with a Maid*, this site would tell me if you had it?"

"The unexpurgated version?" Bozell closed his eyes. "St. Peter's Basilica in London, Ontario. From what the librarian there told me, it has four chapters that were not in the original or any subsequent release. He said that they were 'most disgusting' even for that type of book."

"Monsignor, I am amazed. Both that the Church has a copy of a book I had just made up, that is, the unexpurgated part, but that you knew exactly where it is."

"I have an eidetic memory when it comes to books. It's a useful ability for a librarian. As for the list on the webpage, it's mainly for scholars doing research. They see a work of interest, make an application, and, if approved, we arrange a viewing."

How can a two-thousand-year-old institution be so naïve, Simon asked himself. "Transparency is one thing, Monsignor, but remember, windows are transparent but they allow voyeurs the opportunity to peep into your bedroom. Maybe have the scholars approved then grant them access."

"Yes." Another push of the glasses. "Given what has happened, that might be an idea worth exploring. But the stable doors have been opened and the horses are loose. What's our next step?"

"There are two reasons to steal such a book — money and power. The money aspect is the thief stealing it to sell it to a collector of such works. As for the power, well, is it the kind of book that would allow very nasty people to do even nastier things?"

"Definitely. After discovering its loss I read our digital copy. I can let you read that if it helps."

"You have a copy?"

Bozell nodded. "Yes. We have digital copies of all the works in our care. We use a format exclusive to us, so it can only be read here, on our computers. We keep the files on hard drives in that safe you saw in the library. And no, we do not have a copy of that unabridged novel you mentioned."

"I wasn't going to ask, Monsignor."

"But you were thinking it, Mr. Tombs."

He has me there, Simon thought.

Retrieving the correct hard drive from the safe, he plugged it into the laptop on the table and called up a digital copy of *The Book of Flambeau.*

"This computer does not connect to the internet, Mr. Tombs. It's used only to read the digital books we have on file. As an added precaution, this library was constructed as a massive Faraday cage. All electronic signals are blocked."

"Very smart."

"And for much the same reason, I'd ask you not to take written notes."

"Of course not, Monsignor. Now, if I may?"

"Certainly."

As Bozell busied himself with other duties, Simon began reading. The text was in an older form of French, with which Simon at first struggled. Then he subvocally called up a translation spell, one an old professor had taught him, and began to read easily.

The book was more of a journal, with a different spell, incantation, recipe, curse, or blessing for each day of the year, beginning on March 25th. Margin notes in the same handwriting made it clear that whatever the rite or ritual, it had to be used on the exact date or, at best, it would not work and, at worst, there would be terrible consequences. Simon assumed that this only applied to the occult instructions and not the recipes. He could not imagine a spinach tart tasting better or worse if made on the wrong day unless it was prepared by sorcerous means.

There were, Simon noted, more spells and incantations than domestic tips. And most of those malevolent rather than beneficial.

There was one he noted that came at the beginning of the journal, on a date when Spring would be in full bloom. It was for the renewal of "flagging passion." Did it, he wondered, work only on that day, or did the enchantment last the full year? If the latter, Flambeau could have made himself a very rich man. If the former, then one better make sure to find a willing companion on that date.

Thinking about this caused Simon to begin thinking about the journal as a whole, and its specificity.

Yes, yes, it has to work that way. Why else the calendar format? With this realization, he laughed out loud.

Bozell ran from the vault. "Is something wrong, Mr. Tombs?"

"No, Monsignor, I just realized that *The Book of Flambeau* may not be as dangerous as we first thought. Oh, it's still a very valuable book and I'll do whatever I can to find it for you and the Church. But, well, enough about that. Please have a seat."

When Bozell was sitting opposite him, Simon asked, "What are your views on the contents of a grimoire? Are the words themselves sufficient to cast the spells or curse your enemies, or is it the combination of the words, the book, and the effort, no, make it the *sacrifice* of writing it all down that empowers what is within?"

"That is a good question, Mr. Tombs. I think it is the combination — the book, the words, and the sacrifice. If it were just the words, then, well, there are hundreds if not thousands of versions of the Necronomicon on the internet. Yet, the Old Gods remain banished and Cthulhu still sleeps in R'lyeh."

"But if someone were to hand copy the text?"

"Your 'friends' in the Holy Office have dealt with a few that tried. They all went mad before they copied the first few pages. "

"Thank the Divine for that. Monsignor, I'd like to try something. I don't suppose you could get a printer in here." Bozell shook his head. "I didn't think so. The words on the screen will have to do."

Simon scrolled back to the first page, the one dated "25 March" with no year given. *Of course not. Then he'd have to create a new journal every year.* He concentrated on the opening paragraph, the one in which Flambeau stated the purpose of his work — to do evil and some good; to seduce maidens, married women, and widows; to enrich himself and punish his enemies. The dating was meant to guide him, so he would pace himself and not attempt too much too soon.

Simon stared at this paragraph and studied it until it became a part of him. He then closed his eyes and sent those words out beyond the library, for Faraday had no power over the supernatural. He searched for the words, the written words. He found nothing.

He abandoned his search only when Bozell started shaking him and asking, "Are you all right, Mr. Tombs?"

Simon "awoke" with a "Just fine, Monsignor. I just tried something that didn't work." *And I'll try it again later, writing down the words this time. But there's no need to tell the good monsignor this.* "That's enough for one day. Tomorrow I'll get to work. But for now, what would you say to some before-dinner drinks at Sebastian's followed by dinner at the restaurant of your choice?"

"Sounds good, Mr. Tombs. How about Rosa's? It's an Italian

restaurant of the old school."

"What makes it old school?"

"Priests and their guests eat free."

The next day Simon slept late, the result of one of the finest Italian meals he'd ever eaten. All in all, it had been a fine night — good food, good wine, singing to the songs played by the trio in the corner. *It was worth every penny we didn't pay for it*, Simon thought after he woke and attended to the necessaries. As the monsignor had said, their money was no good at Rosa's. They had, however, left generous tips for their servers.

Over a cup of coffee and one of the bombolones the owner of Rosa's had insisted he take with him, Simon thought of how he might find *The Book of Flambeau*.

He thought about calling Caitlin Hood to ask the detective sergeant if there had been any reports of rare books being stolen. Instead, he called Detective Terence Charm. *I'll do better with Charm. Caitlin would want to know chapter and verse and insist on regular reports. Charm is more practical.*

Simon was right. "Tombs, I'm just going to assume you have a good reason for asking, and that you don't want the sarge to know about it, or you would have asked her. I'll just count this as a favor owed."

After calling Charm, Simon put out feelers among certain people, human and otherwise, regarding any strange supernatural activities, not that he was expecting any, not regarding the book he was seeking. *Still, it can't hurt. Word will no doubt get back to the unholy that I don't like them playing nasty games in my city.*

Then the personal visits. Ginny London of London's Books. Ginny's bookshop was located on the Avenue in the Hampden section of Baltimore. It offered a mix of new and used books, some of the latter rare and collectible. The thief might have inquired about the *Flambeau* before they stole it or tried to sell it to her after the theft.

Simon paused in his planning to think of Ginny. He'd known her in another life, when they both had different names. They had been partners in love and adventure. Their parting was sudden and necessary. He had been Thomas Defreyne for too long, and the dark forces were beginning to catch on.

One day Simon Tombs will have to disappear as well, he sadly reflected, *but that day is still some time off, the Divine willing.*

Simon sometimes wondered if Ginny suspected who he had been. If so, she never said anything. And the most he had ever said about the subject was "The past is passed, Ginny," when she once edged too close to the subject.

That night he would stop in to see Momma Fortuna. Momma operated a small restaurant in Fells Point, the kind where you had to know where it was to find it. It offered reasonably good food and drink at decent prices, but its main appeal was the ever-present card games on the second floor. As a result, Momma seemed to be aware of most of what was going on in Baltimore.

Between these, there was Madison Antiquities. Its owner, Beatrice Newman, had inherited it from her uncle Stuart, who had run it as a museum. Stuart had tried to make a deal with a demon and the result was his messy end. Several of the exhibits Stuart had left Beatrice had been infested or possessed by evil entities. Simon cleared the building of them, after which he and Beatrice had dated for a time. Nothing intimate, just dinners, plays, and movies. They soon stopped seeing each other. Simon was worried that she had spent too much time in the museum alone with demonic entities, and he thought it possible that she blamed him for her uncle's death. (Which he was, albeit not directly.)

Ginny London was a short woman in her mid-70s who had managed to retain most of the figure she had back in the swinging 60s, although time and too much good food had left their marks. Her hair was mostly gray but still had some traces of ginger about it.

When Simon entered the shop, she rushed around the counter

and gave him a big hug. The embrace had more than friendship about it, both of them hugging memories of what had once been.

Once they parted, Ginny went back behind the counter and handed Simon a bag containing books he had ordered.

"Still no *Smuggler's Shuffle*," she said in the slight Midsummer accent she had retained despite decades in Baltimore. "Don't know what's keeping those two from finishing it. Probably busy with other books. Now how can I help you, Simon?"

He told her. Shaking her head, Ginny told him,

"*The Book of Flambeau*. I've heard of it, of course. Nothing good and a nasty piece of work. So, who's lost it?"

Simon shook his head. "I'll tell you about it when I'm done." Some browsing, more purchases, another hug, and he left.

There was a sign on the door of Madison Antiquities. *Out buying oldies but goodies. Be back Thursday.* As it was Tuesday, Simon had a few days to wait. Taking out one of his cards, he left his own note, *See you Thursday. Call if convenient. If inconvenient, call anyway. Simon*, and pushed it through the mail slot.

Momma Fortuna's restaurant was fusion before the term was popular. Having lived and loved for many years, Momma's cooking, and those of her chefs, was a mixture of cuisine from Europe, Africa, Asia, and some places no longer found on maps. Like Ginny had earlier that day, Momma heartily embraced Simon.

"Simon, it's been too long. *She's* not back, is she?"

She was Fel, Simon's former love and companion. At Simon's "No, and I don't think she ever will be," Mamma, not noticing the sadness in his voice, said, "Forgive me, Simon, but I think that's for the best. There was something about her that, well, scared me. And hardly anything does that. But what about that young woman you brought here a few times? You know, the one who dressed all in one color with hair to match? What was her name? Bernadette? Bridget?"

"Beatrice, Momma. And we're just friends." *If that*, Simon added to himself. *I guess I'll find out Thursday.*

Momma shook her head. "You need a woman. If I were only

twenty years younger, or you were ten years older …"

"I doubt I would survive the experience, Momma. I've heard the stories."

Momma laughed. "All true, but at least they died happy. Now, how can I help you? No, wait, eat dinner, leave your waiter a big tip, then go upstairs and play some cards. There's a loudmouth up there and no one would be upset if he went home with empty pockets. Then you can tell me why you came."

So Simon ate, tipped his waiter generously, and cleaned out the loudmouth. After giving Momma half his winnings for the soup kitchen she ran under a different name, he asked her about the *Book of Flambeau.*

"I haven't heard of it. And I guess you can't tell me too much about it. Never mind, I'll mention the name here and there and see who reacts."

❦

Simon spent the next two days going over his plan. He hoped he was right. He prayed he was right. If he wasn't, it was possible that he would not live long enough to correct his mistake. Maybe he would know more after he talked to Beatrice.

Thursday morning, he called Madison's Antiques and spoke to Beatrice. She sounded happy to hear from him and asked him to stop by early afternoon.

Beatrice greeted him wearing all white — pants, sweater, and shoes. Her hair was platinum and there was a pearl ring on her left index finger. He found himself speculating about her hair colors. Were they the result of expensive wigs or excellent dye jobs? If the latter, how far did she go? He was pulled from his speculation by her saying,

"It was a shame how we parted. It's funny how two people who are attracted to one another can drift apart. Maybe after you've accomplished whatever brings you here we can try again."

"I'd like that," Simon replied, not sure if he meant it or was just being polite. He quickly changed the subject. "Any more of your exhibits talking to you?"

"No, thank God. Every one of them is clean and none of them speak. Check if you like."

Simon did and took a moment to open his senses to the shop. There was nothing. There was only a slight sensation coming from Beatrice. Passion? Excitement? Anticipation?

"Everything seems fine."

"Good, now what brings you here? I hope it's me?"

"Have you ever heard of the *Book of Flambeau*? Has anyone come in recently asking about it?"

"No, I don't … no, I'm wrong. A few weeks ago a young man came in. He was young, early twenties, with thin, sandy hair, and scholarly pallor, if you know what I mean." Simon nodded that he did. "He had a list of books that he was looking for, this *Flambeau* might have been on that list. He left me a copy, along with his name and contacts. It's up on my desk, which is a mess. Let me look for it. I'll call you when I find it. In the meantime …"

"When what I'm doing is over, Beatrice. Maybe the second time will be the charm. But for now, as Captain Spaulding once said, I must be going."

Their quick embrace threatened to turn into more but the two parted before it could.

That evening, Simon called Monsignor Bozell. He spent some time questioning the cleric about the Basilica's employees, especially any who worked with him or near the book vault. He then made arrangements to view the digital copy of the *Flambeau* on the following day.

"Monsignor?" Simon asked as Bozell brought up the digital copy then and yielded his seat to him.

"Yes, Mr. Tombs?"

"Does the following person seem at all familiar?" He then described the young man Beatrice said might have been interested in the *Flambeau*.

Bozell thought a moment. "Not that I can say. Many use the

church but I don't come into contact with them. Why, is he our thief?"

"He is, as my police friends would say, a 'person of interest.'"

"Mmmm. Two seminarians have been assigned to me for minor disciplinary action. It seems they were watching videos of the secular Madonna."

"Is that a sin, Monsignor?"

"No, it's often a delight, but not during Mass. Since they like videos so much, I think I'll assign them the task of reviewing our surveillance videos, working backward from when the theft was discovered to, well who can say? It will give them time to rethink their vocations. Now, I will leave you to your research. May it please God that it is successful."

Simon began at the book's start, with Flambeau's caveats about the proper use of his journal and dire warnings about its misuse. These led into a general section, with spells of protection and prayers of worship and obedience. They were, of course, all directed to those who dwell in and rule the Pit, the protection of the spells coming at the cost of one's immortal soul.

A good bargain, Simon thought, *since whoever uses the journal is probably already damned.*

Simon fast-forwarded to the current date, then read each daily entry, stopping on the Tuesday of the following week.

Oh, this might be it and it's a good one. Intense pain followed by sudden death. Just the thing. But I'll have to wait until I hear from Beatrice.

A part of Simon hoped that she'd have no information for him, or that her young man, *and was he "her young man,"* he wondered with a trace of jealousy, would prove to be a crazed collector or the agent of one who just wanted the book to have, hold, and whatever else books collectors do when they're among their treasures.

Time would tell, and in more ways than one, he decided.

Beatrice called the next day.

"Simon, I found the paper the young man gave me about an hour after you left. *The Book of Flambeau* was on his list, along with some books I've never heard of. There's something called *Cthulhu Exponit Omnia* and the rest were the usual — *The Book of Eibon, Les Cultes de Goules,* Seward's *The Undead,* works like that. Anyway, I told him that I had a line on the Flambeau. He was interested and said he'd be here Tuesday. Can you meet with us?"

"Yes, I'd be glad to," Simon lied. Not that he wouldn't meet with them, just that he would not be glad when he did.

On the given day, Simon arrived at Madison Antiques dressed for battle in police-blue cargo pants and a matching camping jacket. In each of his many pockets he had wards, amulets, charms, and weapons both mundane and magical. He held spells and exorcisms in his mind, ready to be released with just a few words, some to be spoken aloud and others just in the mind. He did not expect to need them. That is, he hoped he wouldn't need them.

Simon, you've been wrong before, he told himself before knocking on the locked door of the shop. *And so far you've lived to regret your mistakes.*

He knocked and was answered, Beatrice answering the door wearing all red, from hair to shoes and, presumably, down to her skin.

Her long skirt swished as she stepped aside to let him in. Her breasts brushed against him as she moved to lock the door.

"He's waiting for us in my office."

So, she left him alone.

"He being …?"

"Oh, Joseph Hobbs. A nice young man who's very interested in the *Flambeau.* I think he has information that might help you find it."

"I'm sure," Simon said without inflection then nodded for Beatrice to lead on.

As they walked Simon was alert for any possessed or cursed objects. There were none on the first floor. The paintings on the stairway remained unhaunted, and the more expensive collector pieces on the second floor were also free of taint.

The office then, Simon thought as Beatrice opened its door for him. *Abandon all hope. No, never abandon hope when it might be the only thing you have left.*

Joseph Hobbs was waiting for him, looking just as Beatrice had described. He was holding a book, probably the Flambeau, and standing near the corner where Simon had once banished a Pit demon and from where, or so Simon imagined, other demons had appeared to devour Stuart Newman when they thought he had cheated them.

Simon heard the clicking of locks behind him – one, two, three. There had been only one when he was last there. He looked at Hobbs.

"So it's like that?"

"I am afraid so, Tombs." Hobbs sounded older than he looked. *An old soul in a young body, or a young fool with a deep voice?* "I am aware that you have a talent for doors and locks. So do I, which is how I was able to steal the *Flambeau*. But you won't have the time to use your talent."

Ignoring Hobbs, Simon turned to Beatrice. "Really, is he the best you could do?" he asked, indicating the young man. "What happened, did he wander in and you decided he was the perfect dupe so you seduced him into stealing the book for you?" He glanced at Hobbs. There was something about his expression. "Did you seduce him, or was it payment on delivery?" Another look at Hobbs told Simon his arrow had hit its mark. "Here's a lesson, Joey, whatever the currency, always get paid upfront."

Back to Beatrice. "Why? Is it because you still think I was responsible for your uncle's death."

"You bastard, you were responsible. The voices told me what happened, how you tricked him into betrayal. He was dragged down to Hell, and now you'll join him. I had the book stolen and was going to ambush you with it. No matter. Do it, Joseph, read the curse."

"Just a minute," Simon said. "The condemned man's last words and all that?"

"Go ahead. Not that your words will save you."

"Thank you, Beatrice. Joseph, listen to me. This is your last chance to make the right Choice. Give me the book, walk away, and go on to have a good life. I can recommend a good priest if you have need of one. And you, Beatrice, you have the same Choice. Tell Joseph to give me the book. Being more than a bit in love with you, he'll listen to you."

"Anything else, Tombs?" Beatrice all but sneered at him.

"Just one more thing, as the man in the raincoat always says. What is your real hair color?"

She sighed in disgust. "You had your chance to find out. Joseph, read the damned book."

Hobbs began to read the curse, which was written in a mix of Latin and old French. As he read, Simon felt evil in each word that came from his lips. But that was all he felt – no pain, no suffering, no demons emerging from the shadows to rend his body. Hobbs finished reading. Still, nothing happened.

Hobbs looked at Beatrice. "Wh-what went wrong? I read it correctly, each word carefully pronounced." Beatrice, as surprised as Joseph, had no answer for him.

Simon did. "Your mistake was using a book whose spells were specific to the day. True, that made them powerful enough that I might not have been able to counter them. But the book was written in the late 15th century, under the Julian Calendar. Which means, Joseph, you read the curse about two weeks too late."

Hobbs began flipping pages. "Don't even try, Joseph. As you just told me, you won't have the time. Now if you'll excuse me, I have an alibi to establish."

Quickly, Simon turned to the door and knocked three times. It opened and he stepped through, closing it behind him just as the screaming started.

They should have read Flambeau's warnings, he thought. "But cast a spell wrong and it will return to you with force and you will suffer whatever you wished on another."

The police will find the book, if it isn't destroyed. Detective Charm will connect it to me, and Caitlin will be, well, more than a little upset. I better make a call.

"Monsignor, Simon Tombs. The job is done. But it seems that I might require sanctuary for a few days."

Buyer Beware

Simon Tombs was home, watching the Channel 11 news while eating leftover restaurant food. It was unremarkable chicken parmesan from an equally unremarkable chain Italian restaurant. He normally did not eat at such places but the young lady he was with had insisted.

"It's my favorite place," she told him. "I eat there all the time. I think I've had everything on the menu at least twice."

So, being a gentleman, he deferred to her wishes. The rest of the evening went pleasantly. They ate and boxed up their leftovers then Simon gave her a tour of Baltimore, driving through the historic areas and avoiding those where murders had occurred. A late-night drink at Sebastian's rounded off the evening. As she was staying across the street at the Starry Night, he walked her to her hotel, declining her invitation to stay for breakfast.

"Never again," he said to his boa constrictor Kitty, who had slithered up to him in greeting, "will I allow a vampire to set me up with a blind date. I don't care if she is his human cousin."

He thought about throwing the chicken parm away but hated to waste food. So it became his next day's lunch. But he did not think it was fit for his table, so he ate it on the couch while watching the noon news.

Much of the news was the same as the previous day's, and the previous week's. There was an interesting local item. Activists protesting the increasing automation of grocery and retail stores had hacked the self-checkout computers of the A&P food markets, causing them to insult the customers — mildly swearing at them and mocking their food choices. The protest had backfired, with customers flocking to the stores to be verbally abused as they checked out.

"The best laid schemes and all that," Simon muttered into his lunch. He had just decided that reheating had not improved its taste when the phone rang.

Probably Frederick asking how the date went. Simon wondered if he should lie and if so, by how much? Then he saw who was calling.

"Charm, how are you?"

"Fine, Tombs,"

"What does Caitlin want this time?"

Terrence Charm was a detective for BPD Homicide working for Sergeant Caitlin Hood. Both were very much aware of his "special talents" and called on him when they were needed. He, in turn, sometimes asked favors of them. It was a mutually beneficial arrangement. Simon and Caitlin went back a ways and their relationship could best be described as "rocky," like an on-again/off-again love affair but without the sex. On the other hand, he and Charm were on the road to becoming friends.

"It's a ... well, it's personal this time, Tombs. Listen, if you're not doing anything tonight, how about dinner at my house? I told Molly about you and she's dying to meet you."

Simon looked down at the sad remains of his lunch. "That would be great, Charm."

"Great, around six. Molly wants to know what you'd like her to fix."

"Anything but Italian. I had that last night."

The Charms lived in the Hamilton area of Northeast Baltimore. Theirs was a family-sized house on Arabia Avenue off Moravia Road. It was old and looked as if it might be haunted. *Maybe that's why he called me?* On a whim, Simon opened his senses and scanned it. No ghosts. No negative vibrations at all. Just an overall sensation of peace, love, and happiness. He thought it a big house for just two people and wondered if they were planning on filling it. Charm was only in his forties, maybe Molly was younger. None of his business really.

But if I always minded my business I wouldn't have any fun, would I?

Simon rang the bell. The door opened and …

"You must be Simon. I'm Molly. Wipe your feet and come in."

Molly Charm was best described as "average." She was neither tall or short, thin or otherwise. She was dressed in warm muted shades. Simon presumed she had a figure — everybody does — but as her clothing was long and loose he couldn't tell what kind. He pictured her on the beach — a modest one-piece, a big hat, and a long cover-up. Definitely average.

But there seemed to be something special about her. Warm, friendly, and … magical. No, not magical but certainly something close.

Molly took his coat and walked to the hallway closet. As she did he noticed that her feet did not quite touch the floor.

I wonder if Charm knows.

Charm was waiting for him in the living room. "Thanks for coming, Tombs."

"My pleasure, Charm."

"What's with this Tombs and Charm nonsense? You two sound like characters on a UK streaming channel."

Simon and Charm looked at each other and exchanged the male look that silently said, "Women!" Charm shrugged and said, "It's a guy thing, dear." Which earned him a "humph" in return.

Simon got right to it. "What's the problem?"

Charm's answer was cut off by, "No police talk before dinner. Afterwards, you two can go downstairs and talk business, but not before. Simon, we're having well-done roast beef, baked potatoes, and string beans. I hope that's all right."

"Sounds heavenly, Molly." This got him a look that Charm didn't catch. "Oh, I almost forgot. I had a bag when I came in here."

"You were carrying in when you came in. You put it down when you took off your coat."

"Thanks, you're an angel." Another look. Simon retrieved the bag and handed it to Molly. "Wine for dinner and pastries from the Belair Bakery for dessert."

"Terry, you have to invite Simon for dinner more often. Now, go open the wine and let it breathe. Simon and I will be in a moment."

When Charm was out of the room, Simon asked, "Does he know?"

Molly sighed. "You noticed?" When he nodded, she said, "No, and don't tell him. And if you tell me my cooking is divine I will throw something at you."

"Your secret's safe with me."

"I hear you're good at keeping secrets. By the way, Nika sends her love."

Over dinner, Simon finessed Molly's questions about "his job," her way of getting back at him for his "heavenly" and "angel" remarks, and they segued into talking about TV, movies, and books.

The meal was soon over. "We'll save the pastries for later," Molly decided. Refusing their offer, well, Simon's offer to help clear the dishes, she ordered them to the basement and into the past.

"What the …" was all Simon could say about the knotty pine paneling, the swirled, black 12-inch tile stuck to the floor, and the pool table that dominated the front of the basement. (Charm's workbench and tools accounted for most of the back.)

"Yeah, I know," Charm said. "The last owners didn't do a thing to it when they bought it in the eighties. Me and Molly remodeled the rest of the house, but I wouldn't let her touch this basement. Just wish there was room for a jukebox."

"That's what mp3 players are for."

Charm shook his head. "Not the same, Tombs. Or should I start calling you 'Simon?'"

The two men laughed. Simon said, "I think 'Tombs' and 'Charm' work best for us. Now, what's this all about?"

"Grab some beers, have a seat, and I'll tell you."

Simon got two bottles from a 1950s Frigidaire and joined

Charm on a couch from a more recent era.

"This is new. The old one fell apart one day when me and Molly were … eh, let's just say it fell apart. Now then, it's confession time. Can I assume we're in church?"

Simon knew the expression. To a cop, being "in church" implied a secrecy that went beyond doctor-patient, lawyer-client, or spousal privilege. It went deeper than the confessional and lasted to the grave and beyond.

"As long as it isn't murder, grievous assault, or rape, we're in church."

"Nothing like that. Look, I wasn't the city's best cop. I wasn't the worst but I did things I'm no longer proud of. The sarge has probably filled you in. Nothing really bad, just favors, tip-offs, and turning a blind eye every now and then. Then I met Molly. Knowing her made me take a good, long look at my badge. And for the first time I saw the tarnish on it and decided to start playing it straight. The first thing I did was tell Molly all the bad things I'd done."

"What did she say?"

"That she loved me and trusted me to do the right thing. And if I did that, nothing really bad would happen to me. Since then, I've felt good about myself. That woman saved me, like she was my very own guardian angel."

You don't know the half of it, Simon thought. Then he said, "Let me guess, your past has come back to haunt you?"

"You got that right. It was right before I met Molly. There's this guy, Roger Cormac, you may have read about him in the papers."

"His name's appeared once or twice."

"Well, I was working drugs and I caught this guy, one of Cormac's men, not that we could prove it. He was holding big. Long story short, Cormac made me an offer. A "one-time deal." I made some of the product go away. His guy didn't walk but he did three years instead of the fifteen he should have. That should have been the end of it."

"But it wasn't?"

"Never is. The other day Cormac called me. 'One more favor,' he said. But here's the thing. The favor is, he wants to talk to you."

"Okay, I'll do it."

"What, just like that?"

"Just like that. Why not, we're friends, right? I've met your wife. I've eaten your food. You've saved my life. And besides, if I let anything happen to you, Molly will kill me."

Charm smiled. "I think Caitlin would kill you worse."

I doubt that, Simon thought. He'd seen the vengeance of demons and angels. Of the two, angels were the more terrible, particularly when it came to someone they love.

"Just tell me how I can find this Cormac." Charm gave him a number. "Now then, I think it's time for pastry and coffee. And rest easy. After our business is over, I guarantee Cormac won't ask you for any more favors."

Simon said this last with such finality that Charm almost felt sorry for Cormac. Almost.

The next day Simon called the number Charm had given him. To his surprise, Cormac answered rather than a flunky.

"Tombs, Simon Tombs?"

"Yes, I presume you are the notorious Roger Cormac."

There was a pause then, "I wouldn't say 'notorious,' Tombs."

"Infamous, then. It doesn't matter. I'm surprised you answer your own phone on matters of business."

"Just this phone and just this once. After today, the phone is toast and the number will probably go to some old lady who carries a flip for emergencies only."

"Very smart. Now, when and where do you want to meet."

"Pick a place. One that's safe, if you know what I mean. We don't want anything about our friend on tape."

Let's see, Simon thought. *I don't want this man in Sebastian's. Bartleby's is out as well, one bloodsucker there is enough, even if*

David is open about what he does. Of course, I know the perfect place.

"The Rooftop on the Royale. Given who owns it, I'm sure it's safe. And the noise from the casino will cover our conversation." *And if things go wrong, I can just throw you off the roof.*

"Sounds good. Tonight at nine? Come alone."

"Of course. I don't want any of my friends to see me with you." Simon arrived for the meeting in one of his better suits, one without any concealed pockets. Not that he didn't have a few tricks and a flat-bladed knife up his sleeve. Cormac was in the corner of the balcony bar, near one of the firepits that were keeping the cold at bay. When Simon approached him, a large man in a cheap suit stepped toward him.

"If he tries to frisk me, he will instead fall from a great height and make a mess on President Street. Hopefully, there will be enough left to break your fall when you follow him." At a nod from Cormac, the man backed off. "Now, what do you want?"

"For you to lose the attitude for one thing."

"Too damn bad. Now, I'm here as a favor to Terrence Charm so let's get this done. What do you want?"

"I hear you're some kind of magician or something."

"Let's say I have powers and abilities beyond those of mortal men and let it go at that. Why?"

"There's a ghost in one of my houses."

"And what do you want me to do about it?"

"What else, get rid of it."

"Did you put it there?"

"What's that supposed to mean?" Simon didn't answer, just stared. Finally, Cormac got his meaning.

"Listen, I bought that house about ten years ago. My uncle had just died and my aunt needed a place to stay. It was a nice house in a nice neighborhood, a little big for her but I had people watching over her. When she died last year I had the house fixed up, put it on the market, and it sold. Now the people who bought it say they're seeing ghosts."

"So, give them their money back."

"I did, and then some. They're family of some … friends of mine so no problem with that. Even had my realtor find them someplace nicer. But I want you to look into it. If the place is really haunted or there's something else wrong I want you to fix it."

"And if it's clean?"

"Then I put it back on the market and you and me are done."

"You mean, you and Terrence Charm are done. I'm doing this a favor for him."

"I don't know. I might need another favor one day."

Simon had been expecting something like this and was ready. Taking a deck of cards and an envelope from his suit coat, he opened the deck and fanned the cards in front of Cormac.

"Pick a card, any card."

"Okay, I'll go along." Cormac drew out a card.

"Without showing me the card, seal it in the envelope and put the envelope on the table."

Cormac did, asking "Now what? I tell you my card, look in the envelope and there it is?"

"Not exactly."

The envelope suddenly burst into flames. As Simon, Cormac, and a nervous waiter watched, it burned away, leaving only a card. But it was not the six of diamonds that Cormac had drawn. It was a Tarot card lying face down on the table. The card was not burnt or singed.

"Go ahead, turn it over."

Cormac did so, revealing the image of Death.

"What the hell does this mean?"

"It's a warning to leave Terrence Charm alone."

"And if I don't?"

"Then it's a promise. Now, what's the address of this house?"

The next morning, Simon called a realtor who owed him a

few favors. Cormac's wasn't the first haunted house Simon had cleared out. He asked the woman to look up the history of the house. She called back in two hours.

"The house is about eighty years old. Like a lot of houses in old northwest Baltimore, a wealthy family built it, then sold it when the neighborhood started changing. Jews then blacks caused most of the original owners to move further north on Park Heights and Reisterstown. They didn't stop until they crossed the county line.

"This house you asked about went through a few owners. Oddly enough for that area, it wasn't cut up into apartments. The last owner was a Mavis McConnell. Before that were the Holts, Karl and Nina. They lived there about forty years."

"Why did they move?"

"Karl disappeared. Nina sold it and moved in with her sister. That's when Mavis McConnell moved in. When she died, the house went to Roger Cormac. Then it was sold but the sale was canceled after about a month and the purchase price refunded. Listen, Simon …"

"Yes, Shana?"

"The money that fled sixty years ago is now moving back. Big houses, low prices. They're forcing the people they once fled from back into the city. The people who canceled that sale must have a good reason because within ten years, homes in that area are going to double in price, if not triple. If it's on the market I could put in a bid for you."

"Let me think about it. I might just check it out."

From what Shana told him, Simon had a good idea of who the ghost might be. Still, it was early days and there could be any number of reasons for a spirit in residence. Since Cormac had given him the key, he decided to check it out.

Simon pulled off Reisterstown Road and onto Kenshaw Avenue just as the sun was going down. One does not hunt ghosts in the daytime. Before going in, he looked it over — big yards in the front and back. The ground was neat — grass cut, leaves raked, bushes and trees trimmed.*Cormac must use a service. Wonder if any of them had a fatal lawnmower accident.* Simon thought about all the yard work involved and could not imagine himself cutting grass or shoveling snow. *Escalating prices or not,* he thought. *I'm staying in the city.*

He pictured the inside of the house — living room, dining room, probably a family room along with a huge kitchen. At least four bedrooms on the second floor and, yes, an attic. Storage or another bedroom. Simon figured the former and wondered if there was a body or two hidden in the floor or walls. Maybe Nina had tucked Karl's body away before moving to her sister's.

Simon wondered if Karl and Nina had had any children. He hoped so. Like Charm's, this house was made for a large family. *Will Charm and Molly ever have any? I guess it depends on how human she's allowed herself to become.*

Despite her nature, Fel's body had been completely human. Sighing in regret of what might have been, Simon got out his key. The door opened before he could use it.

First time that's happened without my asking, he thought. *I guess I'm expected. Oh well, as the man in the cape said, "Enter freely and of your own free will."*

Trying not to think about how well that worked out for Jonathan Harker, Simon entered, glad for the spirit knife and the other items he carried.

Simon stood just inside the front door and scanned the house. There was something in the family room to his left. He walked in and looked around. Nothing, and yet, something. Then, near a card table and a couple of chairs, the air became hazy. Slowly, the haze took human form and sat in one of the chairs.

It, he, was a small black man in his sixties. If alive, he'd probably been about 170 and five-eight or nine. Simon got the impression that when younger he might have been a little taller and heavier, an athlete or soldier who'd shrunk with time. He was wearing a blue plaid shirt with tan chinos. The man smiled and waved in greeting.

"Karl Holt?" Simon asked.

Holt nodded and moved his arm in a "gimme time" gesture. Finally, he let out a croak and said, "Forgive me, sir, it takes a minute for my speech to kick in. How come you're not running away like the last ones did?"

Simon smiled. "I ain't afraid of no ghosts."

Holt gave out a laugh. "Yeah, I saw that movie too. All of them. First one was the best but they were all good. I guess you're the guy they sent to get rid of me."

"Depends. May I sit?"

The ghost nodded. "Yeah, have a seat. Such as it is. This table and these chairs are all that's left. They done cleaned everything else out. Now you were saying about something depending?"

"I don't like the guy who sent me but he's got a friend of mine by the shorts. Maybe we can work something out."

"Maybe we can, Mr. …?"

"Tombs, Simon Tombs, mage, miracle worker, and busybody. Call me Simon."

"Pleased to meet you, Simon. I'm Karl. I'd shake hands but, well, you know. That takes some effort."

"Tell me your story, Karl."

"Well, Simon, ain't much to tell. Married my Nina right after getting out of the army. Did mechanic work wherever they sent me. I was good at it, could fix anything with a motor whether you flew it or drove it. So when I got out and me and Nina got married, I always had work. A man good with tools always has work, less he's lazy, or a drinker, or a doper and I was none of them. I was a lover in my younger days, and sometimes in the army, and still was after I got married, but only with Nina mind you." Karl laughed again.

"We did good, Nina and me. Bought this house, raised four good kids and sent them out into the world. They had sense enough to leave Baltimore but they kept in touch with me and Nina. I hope they stuck by Nina after I was killed."

Simon noted the "killed" but didn't say anything, letting Karl talk.

"One day these two men come to the door and say they want to buy my house. Said there was this lady who saw it and liked it. Now with the kids gone Nina and I had been talking about moving, maybe to a condo or something. Some place with elevators, you know. But we weren't ready yet. And I told them so. One of them, they were both ugly, white men but this one was the uglier, said that was a shame because this lady really liked the house. I told him that there were other houses probably just as nice. Neither him or the less ugly one had anything to say, not even, 'Thank you for your time.' They just left.

"Now that was the first of my last two mistakes. I should have known them for who they were and taken whatever they offered. There were only two kinds of big, ugly, white men who'd come into this neighborhood that time of night, and neither one was a cop. I never got a chance to realize that was a mistake.

"I got grabbed the next day on my way to work. I worked at Keruly's Auto Repair down on Wabash. Never made it that day. First day I missed in ten years.

"I don't remember much after that. I woke up in the woods somewhere, looking for where they buried my dead body. That's when I remembered my last mistake."

"Which was?" Simon prompted.

"When they were beating me, I said something like, 'I ain't gonna rest until I get justice.' And I haven't really rested since then. Not in peace like I should have. My spirit wandered for a time in those woods, sometimes scaring druggies and lovers, until I found myself back home. A white woman was living there by then. Well, if you could call it living. She had servants for cooking and cleaning, and nurses to watch over her, but she was mostly alone. I felt sorry for her, even though she was mainly the reason I was dead and Nina was … well, I didn't know. Still don't."

"She sold the house and moved in with her sister."

"With Dolly, well good for her. Dolly was nice. Say, once this is over and if I'm still around, could you find out …"

"I'll do what I can, Karl. About this woman?"

"Mavis McConnell. She's the one who moved in. Like I said, she was lonely. I felt for her. So one day while she was in this very room watching television, I sort of … appeared and let her see me. I figured if she screamed I'd disappear real fast and she'd think she'd been seeing things."

"But she didn't scream?"

"No, sir. She scrunched up her face, smiled, and said, 'Took you long enough. I felt something about three months ago. What are you doing in my house?'

"I told her that before it being her house it was my house. She got this weird look on her face and said, 'Sorry' and that's all either one of us ever said about that. What she said next was, 'I guess you can stay then,' and offered me the room next to hers if I needed it. Well, I didn't really but thanked her anyway and I did use it from time to time.

"After that, I'd show up in the evening and we'd watch the television or talk about the old days and how they were better than these days and neither of us was as lonely as we had been.

"Then one day, it must have been about two years after I 'moved' in, Mavis — we had started out 'Miss Mavis' and 'Mr. Holt' but soon agreed that was just silly — Mavis, she asked if I ever 'looked in' on her when she was sleeping, or changing clothes, or taking a bath. I told her the truth, that I never had, that a gentleman did not do that unless invited. She smiled and said, 'Consider yourself invited.' After that, well, once we figured out how to do certain things, we were both *a lot* less lonely. I remember the first time after we'd 'figured things out' she woke up and found me still in bed with her. She said, 'Oh, you're still here?' I asked her where else would I be. And she said, 'I heard that when you lay a ghost it disappears.' Only dirty joke I ever heard her tell but it was a good one.

"After that, we were like an old married couple. Until the end, that is. She died in her sleep, with me watching over her. I wasn't sure if she'd appear next to me or move on. She moved on and I was glad for her but sad for me."

"What about the new people?"

"Sandy and Sandy. That's right. He was named Sanderson and her Sandra. I didn't like them but I couldn't leave, could I?"

"So you decided to make them leave?"

He laughed again. "Yeah. I'd show up at dinner time and sit in one of the chairs. Or I'd change the channel when they watched TV. Mavis taught me how to do that. And can you imagine how you'd feel if you stepped out of the shower to find an old black man staring at your naked body?"

"Sandra?"

"Hell no. I'm a gentleman, remember? Sanderson. And boy did he scream, just like a girl. They moved out the next day. And I guess that's why you're here. You're here to lay the ghost, and not in the good way. That knife you've got in your pocket would probably do it."

"You can feel that?" Karl nodded. "It might, Karl. It might rend your soul to pieces. But it might not. That whole not resting until you get justice thing binds you to this place. So let me ask, what, to you, would be justice?"

Karl thought for a moment. "Bible says an eye for an eye and all that."

"So you'd want the one responsible beaten to death?" Before Karl could answer, Simon asked, "What would Nina say? What would Mavis say? They wouldn't like it. Neither would the Ones who have claimed vengeance for Themselves. You may get your vengeance only to wind up someplace far from the women you love. So I ask you the Question, Karl Holt. What, to you, is Justice?"

Karl thought long and hard, then made his Choice. Simon smiled in approval.

🍸

A bar on Dundalk Avenue somewhat into Baltimore County. It didn't have a name, unless one counts the neon signs in the window, one of which says "Bar" and the other "Package Goods."

Most of its customers just call it "the corner bar" even if it is just up the corner from where a no-name grocery store stands.

This is where Simon told Cormac to meet him.

Simon was dressed for the place in black, faded jeans, above the ankle work boots (steel-toed of course), a flannel shirt, and a squall jacket. Cormac wore a black overcoat over a dark suit. Not exactly off the rack but nothing that would get him noticed.

"This place is a dump," Cormac complained when he found Simon sitting with his back against a corner wall.

"Yes, it is, but it's a clean, friendly dump, and best of all it's, as you would say, safe."

Cormac looked behind him. "Where's my guy?"

"Being detained outside by Detective Charm. I think they call it a 'stop and frisk.'"

"What if there's trouble?"

"Charm has instructions to shoot your man then come in and help me. Seriously, there's trouble here every other night. County cops not only know all the bartenders by their first names but also most of the patrons. There's one officer who's dating two of the barmaids at once."

Cormac snuffed out a laugh. "Isn't that somewhat dangerous?"

Simon shrugged. "She's a tough cop. She can handle herself, and them. But we're here to talk about ghosts. Rather one ghost."

"It's gone then?"

"No, he's not. There are two options. I wanted to see which one you like better."

"Okay, what are they?"

"Well, once upon a time ..." Over beers, Bulfinche's Pale Ale on tap, Simon told Cormac what Karl Holt had told him, all except how Karl and Mavis had "figured things out." Even without that bit of information, the longer Simon spoke the angrier Cormac got. When Simon finished his story, Cormac all but hissed, "What are the options?"

"I know several people — a few couples, two triads, and the rest singles — who would love to buy a house inhabited by a friendly ghost. They'd probably consider him part of the family, just as your aunt did. In fact, there would likely be a bidding war and you'd wind up selling the house for much more than your asking price. That's your first option."

Another hiss. "And the second one?"

"There's a way of getting rid of Karl Holt but there's a cost."

"Whatever the price, I'll pay it. That son of a bitch refused to sell me the house my aunt wanted then once he was gone, he moved in with her, haunted her, God knows what he did to her."

Cormac started shouting. People started staring. As he paused to contain himself, Simon thought, *Well, I know, so I'm sure They know, and as the two were in love, They no doubt approved.*

Once he was calmer, Cormac went on. "And that dead bastard had the nerve to drive out the people I sold the house to. You talk about cost? I had to pay a premium on top of the refund just to keep them quiet. So you can bet your magical ass that whatever the cost of getting rid of that damned ghost is I'll pay it."

Simon took a deep breath. "Just to be clear. Roger Cormac, I ask you this Question. Are you willing to pay the cost of removing the spirit of Karl Holt from the house where he is dwelling?"

Without hesitation, Cormac said. "Hell yes, I'll pay it. I want that dead bastard out of my house and gone from this world."

Simon nodded. He had expected no less. "The Choice is made. Meet me at midnight tomorrow at the house."

"Why do I have to be there?"

"It's your house. You have to be there to seal the deal."

"All right then."

The next day, thirty minutes before midnight. Simon and Karl were sitting at the card table, waiting.

"I checked on Nina, Karl."

"And?"

"She passed away about four years ago. Cancer got her. But

she died peacefully in her sleep with her family there to send her off."

"I wish I could've …"

"You'll see her soon."

"Yeah, but what if Mavis is there too?"

"I'm sure you three will 'figure things out.'"

"If we do, that will be Heaven."

The bells of the nearby churches were tolling midnight when the front door opened and Roger Cormac walked in.

Simon stood and called out, "We're in here." Cormac joined them in what had been the family room. Karl then stood and walked up to him,

"Mr. Cormac, before I died I swore I'd never rest until I got justice. Now you done me all kinds of wrong. You stole my life. You stole my house. But for circumstances, you would have condemned me to an eternity of loneliness. But if you apologize for everything you done to me, I'll consider that justice served and move on."

Karl extended his hand, causing Simon to think, *You're a better man than I am, Karl. Let's see what happens.*

"What about it, Mr. Cormac?"

Cormac's reply was short, vulgar, and physically impossible, even for a ghost.

Karl looked at Simon and shrugged. "Well, I tried."

"That you did. Say hello to Nina and Mavis for me."

"I'll do that, Simon. Thank you for everything."

Karl walked forward, his body passing through Cormac. As he absorbed Cormac's life essence, the man started to fade.

"What the …" Karl asked once he was fully solid. Then, "Oh yeah, it makes sense. You have to be alive again to die again." Then his lifeless body collapsed. In seconds, it had faded away.

"What the hell just happened?" Cormac asked as he looked through his body.

"That's the Cost you agreed to pay. For Karl to move on, someone had to take his place."

"But you didn't tell me that."

"You didn't ask. Buyer beware and all that. Enjoy being alone, because I'll make sure this house is never sold. That it stays empty forever. And if it falls apart or gets torn down, its ghost will remain for you to inhabit."

"For how long?"

"Who can say? Maybe one day you'll repent your sins, be forgiven, and move on. If not, and you really want out …"

Simon walked over to the card table. From his pockets, he took the Death card that he had shown Cormac and placed it on the table. From his sleeve, he drew his ghost knife and stabbed the card with it. Slowly, the card absorbed the knife.

"If you ever want out, tap the card. The knife will flow from it to you, rend your soul, and send you to wherever you deserve to be. I recommend seeking forgiveness and redemption."

With that, Simon left the house. Cormac tried to follow but could not cross the threshold.

Simon looked back at him. "You should have apologized."

The next morning Simon called Detective Charm. "Problem solved, favor done, and, as promised, Roger Cormac will never bother you again."

"You didn't … no, I don't want to know. Thanks, Tombs, I owe you big."

"Friends don't keep score, Charm. Next time, dinner's on me at Rosa's."

Blood Dance

Simon Tombs was awake. For the past week or so he had not slept for more than an hour or two a night. It had happened before. It was his body's reaction to doing too much in too little time. Meditation helped, but what he needed were a few weeks of inactivity.

He thought about spending a few weeks at the luxury condominium he had in Ocean City. Watching the sun rise and set. Sitting on the beach while watching the waves and feeding already fat seagulls. Afternoon naps. Walking the Boardwalk and buying tacky souvenirs and tee-shirts for his friends. Eating dinner at a different restaurant every night. Then the night spots. There had to be a few that featured music that he liked, or at least had heard before.

Maybe Charm could get some time off and he and Molly could join me. Caitlin and her friend … Betty? Britanny? No, Barbara. They could come as well. We'd make a rule that there would be no shop talk and break it the second night and tell stories about dead bodies, weird accidents, drunks who sank boats, and things like that. Maybe I'd get a chance to talk with Molly, learn more about why she's taking a break from …

The phone rang. With the life he led, at this late hour it could be any of a dozen people. The caller was none of them.

"Detective Payne, how are you?"

"Fine, Mr. Tombs. First of all, I'm sorry about what happened last week at Sebastian's. I didn't know how strong that drink was."

"You shouldn't have more than one of anything called 'Cthulhu Happens.'"

"Yeah, and I had three. So, sorry for any disturbance."

"Don't worry about it. I understand yours was the finest

performance of "A Policeman's Lot" anyone's heard in a long time. Sometime later you'll have to tell me about your connection with Gilbert and Sullivan. I'll buy. For now, why are you calling me this late at night, or rather, this early in the morning?"

"We need your help, Mr. Tombs. We have a dead vampire."

Simon could only think of David. "Where?"

Timothy Payne gave Simon an address in Harbor East. David's condo. He considered asking about David's human companion Robert, then thought better of it. The less the police knew about his connection with David the better.

"I'll be right there. Just give me time to dress."

"I'm not interrupting anything, am I?"

"Sadly, no." *There hasn't been anything to interrupt since Christmas*, Simon reflected. *Another reason to go on vacation. Maybe I won't ask Charm and Caitlin.*

David's condo was so exclusive it did not have a name, just the street address in large numbers on the front. Anyone who did not know what the building was was not considered worthy of living there. David liked living large, if "living" could be properly applied to a vampire.

David had the top floor, harbor view. When he got off the elevator, Payne was there to meet him.

"Thanks for coming."

"A dead vampire, why wouldn't I?"

Standing in the doorway, Simon visually and mentally scanned the apartment. A police ram had been used to force the front door. The kitchen and living room were neat, no struggle there, and there were no traces of magic or any supernatural activity. The bedroom then, where a uniformed officer was standing with a clipboard. The crime scene.

Simon wondered one thing. How did the police get in? Vampires are very protective of their lairs. One needs permission to enter, even by force. Then he realized that if the vampire was dead, it no longer mattered.

He turned to Payne. "May I?"

For David's sake, he'd follow the age-old rules and ask permission. He almost expected to hear, "Enter freely and of your own will." Instead, Payne replied, "Of course, that's why I called you."

Simon nodded and went in.

It was Robert, not David. He was on the bed he and David shared lying on his back, arms spread out, wearing a blue suit with a yellow shirt, no tie. The shirt had been torn open and there was a stake protruding from his chest.

Simon's first thought was, *Oh David, what have you done?* Then to Payne he said,

"He's not a vampire."

"Are you sure? I mean, with the blood and the stake and all. Baltimore's a creepy place, what with all that went down with the Ripper in the garage. I just thought …"

"Vampires exist, Detective, but this isn't one of them. When the undead are staked, there's no blood, not as we know it. And the stake only holds them in place so you can cut off their heads or burn them to ashes, preferably both. Silver kills them as well. Once dead, their age catches up with them and they crumble into dust."

Simon wanted to get close and touch the stake to see what it told him. But he knew how sensitive people, or rather, the crime scene people were about the handling of evidence. He moved closer.

The stake resembled a movie prop, fifteen inches long, two inches wide at the top, tapering down to the point buried in Robert's chest. Simon extended his senses.

There was … nothing. The stake was just another piece of wood, with no feeling of malice or passion coming from it.

The killer is a practitioner, Simon thought. *They masked their work. There's no way to track them. Wait …*

"There's not enough blood," he said aloud more to himself than anyone else. The observation caused him to probe further, ignore the stake, and go deeper. There was something there but what?

Dammit, I'm a magician, not a doctor.

Simon stepped away from Robert. Then, for the first time since seeing his body, he wondered where David, the true vampire in this case, was.

"What can you tell me?"

Simon looked up and saw that Payne had been watching him. There were others with him, fellow detectives, crime scene people in their black cargo pants, grey polo shirts, and equipment vests.

Too many.

"Not here," he told Payne. "Tomorrow morning. At Sebastian's."

The detective understood. "It's a date. Is there anything you can give me right now?"

"Yes, tell the ME to look past the stake."

"What the hell does that mean?"

"I wish I knew. It's just a feeling."

Dawn was about three hours away. As he drove home, Simon wondered if David, not knowing what had happened, might suddenly appear on the scene. Given David's nature, "appear" could have any one of several meanings. He worried that the vampire might mistake the scene and attack the police.

That could get messy, Simon thought. *I should have stayed. What if … No, David's no fool and it's likely that he felt the bond between him and Robert break. If he didn't break it himself. No, if he had, there would not have been a body to find. I hope he has a bolt hole because he's not going to sleep on his special sheets tonight.*

When Simon got home, he had no sooner hung up his coat when,

Tap, tap, tap.

The noise came from outside his balcony door, fingers on glass. "'Tis some visitor," he muttered, "taping at my balcony door." He allowed himself to hope it was Fel, returning to him from lands far off with great stories and adventure to tell him, with maybe a few visible scars and some not so visible that she'd show him later.

No, she was not the kind to tap. She'd be more likely to sneak in when he was asleep and joyously wake him up. No, Simon knew who it was, who it had to be.

Simon slid open the door to find a true creature of the night. Dark skin, darker clothing, a shadow so black that if he had wings he could be Poe's Raven. But vampires don't have wings. That much about them was a myth.

"David," Simon said in a sour greeting. His being there was a breach of their unspoken agreement.

"Simon."

"I'm not going to invite you inside."

"I would not expect you to." Before Simon could ask, David said, "I need your help."

"It's about Robert, isn't it?" Simon asked. "You know?"

"Yes," came the voice in the darkness. Simon tried to gauge its tone. Angry? Sad, Worried? He couldn't tell.

Simon gestured to one of the chairs, sure that the vampire could see him do so. "Have a seat. Can I get you something? Sweet Tea, coffee, orange juice? I have Bulfinche's on tap. I'm afraid the only blood I have is inside me and I'd like to keep it there."

"No, nothing. That favor you owe me. I'm calling it in."

"David, before you speak, I have to ask. Did you kill him? Did he turn and you had no choice?"

There was sadness in the vampire's voice when he answered, "No. This is not … my work. My fault, maybe, not my doing."

"His enemies or yours?"

"Mine," David said quietly. "Word reached me about a new vampire in the city, one looking to take my place. I do not know who he is or where he rests. He probably killed Robert to get my attention. I need your help to find him and to destroy him."

Him? Could be a her, Simon thought. *Or even a they.* "First of all, I am sorry about Robert. I know he was close to you."

In the dark, the vampire shrugged. "Yes, I suppose so. I tell myself there were others before him and, when this is over, another will take his place. Humans, it's hard when you become attached to them."

From the way he said it, David could have been talking about a pet he had had to put down. What was it the little girl in black said about homicidal maniacs? That they look like everyone else? Simon supposed that applied to monsters as well. He had forgotten that, despite his appearance, the creature on his balcony had not been human for over three hundred years.

"I was watching from the opposite rooftop. I know you've been to the scene. Can you trace the killer?"

"Not in this case. Whoever did this was very careful not to leave anything for me to track. How did you find out?"

"I was out feeding. I came in through the bedroom window as I do most nights." A slight pause. "I saw him and just stood there. I don't know for how long. I heard voices in the hallway, then pounding on my door and people shouting 'Police. Open up!' I left the way I came in. They forced the door, didn't they?"

"Yes, but I don't understand how. 'Enter freely and all that.'"

"The apartment is, was, in Robert's name. The police will find nothing to identify or incriminate me. As for their getting in, when I left him lying there, I knew I'd not be back. Having abandoned my home, it was no longer mine and so anyone could enter if they had the will and the means."

"About the stake. Any chance you recognized it?" It was something to ask. Simon was not expecting any answer beyond "No" or a shrug.

"Yes, it was mine."

"Yours? Why does a vampire …"

"Own a stake. Dark humor, I suppose. A reminder that no matter how strong we are or how long we've lived, we're not immortal. I acquired this one back in the late 1800s. It was in the chest of the Baltimore before me.

"Back then, where there were vampires there were vampire hunters. These days, the kin are more careful and most people don't believe in us, so there are no more vampire hunters, none that specialize that is. But back then, one of the hunters found Baltimore and staked him so that the rising sun would destroy him."

Simon suspected he knew the answer, but he asked anyway. "What did you do?"

"Watched him burn. Then I slept. The next evening I retrieved the stake and became the new Baltimore. It's the way of things. If you're not strong enough, someone replaces you. So far, despite a few who thought I wasn't, I've been strong enough."

"And this new challenger?"

"With your help, he'll go the way of the rest."

"I'll find who killed Robert. The rest is up to you."

"That's all I ask. Who do you think called the police?"

Simon had wondered this himself. "A neighbor who heard noises, maybe Robert's screams. Or your rival waited until you returned then called them hoping you'd be found with the body. Do you have a place to go?"

"I have a few places. Forgive me if I don't tell you where. I wouldn't want you to lie to the police when they question you." The sky was starting to lighten. "It will be dawn soon. I had better go." With that, he was gone.

As David faded away, Simon said to the night, "Damn, I was hoping to watch him turn into a bat."

The next morning, Simon met with Detective Payne at Sebastian's. Both men had been awake all night and so had ordered the strongest coffee available.

"There's always Hotter Chocolate," Simon suggested.

"No thanks, I'm on duty. When this is over, I'm gonna try a hotter Cthulhu and see what happens. But for now, let's get down to business. What do you know about the dead guy?"

"Write this down because your recorder won't work. I knew the victim only as Robert. I met him a few times in a club on

Charles Street called Bartleby's. It does not serve alcohol but the wait staff doesn't ask questions about what might be added from brown paper bags. Whenever I saw him, Robert was in the company of someone named David."

"And David is …"

"A vampire." Simon paused to give Payne time to absorb this information and adjust his belief systems.

"You're not shitting me, are you, Tombs? I mean you're talking about an honest-to-God, blood-sucking, risen-from-the-grave vampire?"

"Yes, and I'm not sure if David is his real name or just one he goes by. He and Robert were in a relationship."

"You mean they were lovers?"

Simon thought about David. The David he thought he knew and the one he'd talked to the previous night. "I don't know. Maybe David loved him as much as much as a soulless creature can love anyone. I know he fed off Robert a few times each month. What else they did was none of my business. There were others who, freely and of their own will, allowed David to feed off them."

"Are any of these 'others' vampires?"

"No, but they are out there."

"How many?"

"I don't know. Less than you'd expect, more than you can handle."

Payne let out a sigh and signaled for another cup of coffee. "Okay, prior to last night, were you ever in the apartment those two shared?"

"Last night was the first time. For obvious reasons, I made sure I knew where he lived, if that's the right word for an undead vampire, but I never had cause to go there."

"Okay, one more thing. When was the last time you saw this David."

"On the night in question, I spoke with him outside my apartment. He told me he was innocent and asked me to find Robert's killer. He left before I could make any attempt to restrain him."

"How did he leave?"

"He disappeared." Before Payne could ask, Simon added, "He's a vampire. That's what they do. Now, here's my one more thing.

"David is a vampire. He should be considered extremely dangerous if cornered. No, he should be considered deadly. I don't know how many of your officers it would take to bring him down, but I don't think you have enough. The only things that will kill him are silver, beheading, and immolation. Oh, and exposure to sunlight. But I've told you that. Sacred objects are only effective if the person wielding them truly believes."

"Anything else?"

"I would appreciate your forwarding me any and all reports. Given the nature of who and what we're dealing with, I may see something you won't."

"Makes sense."

And take this." Simon handed Payne a card.

"What is this?"

"It's the number of the Hi-Ho Mining Company in Arizona. They sell all things silver."

Basil's Bar & Grill was a small bar off Urbana Pike in Frederick County. It had been there for as long as anyone could remember. Many a young person had had their first drink in Basil's. And its dark parking lot nightly bore witness to squeaky shocks and steamy windows. It was that kind of a place. And it was owned by a vampire.

"So you're Basil?" Simon asked the owner.

"Have been for seventy years now." The small, thin person in a neat grey suit smiled. "Of course, that's not my name. It was the name of the original owner. He died just before I took over. Natural causes in case you're wondering, Mr. Tombs."

"I wasn't, and even if I were I would not have asked."

"I didn't think you would. Thank you for the tip about the company that makes fabric from soil. Sleeping on sheets is much more comfortable than dirt."

"They make pajamas too. I found out about them from Baltimore. Speaking of whom …"

"Yes, I thought that's why you called me. I don't know where he is, and I probably would not tell you if I did."

"That's not why I asked to meet you. When I need David, eh, Baltimore, I'll find him. How much do you know about the death of his companion?"

The vampire known as Frederick, after the county which he "ruled," shook his head. "Not much, just that he died under suspicious circumstances." Simon filled Frederick in. "So you think …"

Simon took a sip of whatever tap beer he'd been served. "Three possibilities. David killed Robert in a crime of passion."

"I can't imagine Baltimore getting passionate about anything."

"Neither can I, but it can't be ruled out. And he certainly would not have called the police. When we talked, he mentioned that there was another of your kind who wanted to take his place as Baltimore. Have you heard of anyone looking for a … new position."

"No, but it's possible. If so, it's not a smart move. Why warn your target? What's your third possibility?"

"A fearless vampire hunter who mistook Robert for David. Which is why I wanted to meet with you, to make you aware. The next attack may come during the day, either for real or as a feint."

"I see. Thank you for that, Mr. Tombs. I shall advise the other kin to take care of themselves and those under their protection. And if there are any other … occurrences, you will be the first to know."

"Just make sure you take photographs before you dispose of the bodies."

"Our bodies dispose of themselves, Mr. Tombs."

"I thought so, but I wanted to be sure."

Simon slept most of the day. When he awoke he began his search, starting with the obvious.

"Police beat you here," Herman, the bartender and owner of Bartleby's told him.

"Sorry about that," Simon said.

Herman shook his head. "No worries. They would have been by eventually. Shame about Robert. I didn't know him that well and that's what I told them, that he was David's shadow. That he never came in by himself. That David did and usually left with somebody else. We all knew what that was about. It was no secret what David was and this was one of the places to come if you were into that scene."

"Did you tell that last to the police?"

Herman shook his head. "Didn't have to. That Detective Payne knew what was what. When he came in, he asked if I had A-positive on tap. When I gave him a funny look, he quietly flashed his badge, told me about Robert, and asked about David. I answered his questions, he paid for coffee he didn't order and I didn't serve, and started to leave."

"Started to? Let me guess, there was one more thing."

Herman smiled. "Yeah, there always is. That man in the raincoat has a lot to answer for. He asked if I ever saw anyone paying too much attention to them, or leave just after they did like they were following them."

"Did you?"

"Simon, I'll tell you the same thing I told Payne. That my job is to serve the customers and keep soft music playing. It's not to keep track of who is coming and going, unless it looks like they're going to come in one of the back booths."

Simon smiled at the joke. "Is there anyone who used to come in, particularly when David and Robert, or just David, did, but hasn't been in for a week or two."

"Hmm, Payne missed that one. You don't think …"

"I'm not thinking. Right now I'm fishing with no bait in a dead lake hoping for a miracle catch. If you do remember anyone like that, or anyone who left with one of David's regulars, give me a call."

Simon dropped his card and two fifties on the service counter. "Drinks for the house. Save some for yourself."

Simon had an advantage over Payne and his fellow detectives. He knew the places where those who preferred the darkness and the night gathered. Every part of the city had one or two. Most were not advertised. Those who needed to know knew. Most of the time he arrived before the police. When he did, he gave the owners the news about Robert, told them that the police might arrive, and suggested they be nice to the detectives who were only doing their job.

One man, a nasty sort who called himself Bodsworth and who ran an after-hours bar in an abandoned store in the ruins of Oldtown Mall asked, "And what if I'm not?"

"They will probably shut you down, take you in, confiscate your stock, and drink it themselves. If they don't, I'll have to come back and do my job, won't I?" Simon replied menacingly.

"They'll have my full cooperation, Mr. Tombs."

Simon spent the rest of the night "fishing" without getting so much as a nibble. The next night looked as if he'd have the same result. But sometimes even a dead lake can have a fish or two in it.

It was three a.m. and the night was dark. It was cloudy and a new moon. The place was called "Late Night Reads." It was a below-the-street place on Harford Road just north of Hamilton Ave. It shared basement space with a truly underground unofficial movie theater, which had late-night to early-morning viewings of videotapes that had been salvaged from old video rental stores.

Late Night Reads was divided in two. The front was a bar with tables — wine before two, coffee, tea, and hot chocolate afterwards. The back was a bookshop with shelves lining the wall and comfortable chairs in the middle. There was a five-dollar cover charge for the bookshop. This allowed you to take a book from the shelves, sit quietly, and carefully read it. If you decided to buy the book, the five dollars went toward its purchase price. For some of its patrons, it was a place of refuge. For a few, it was the only home they had. All were welcomed as long as they didn't snore too loudly.

Simon knew about Late Night Reads and went there when he needed to think without being disturbed. But going there made him feel like he was cheating on Ginny and her bookstore so he did not go there often.

Simon paid his five dollars, donated another twenty, and asked the usual questions of Selwyn Krist, the shop's owner.

"I don't remember seeing this David you described, but I do know, or did know Robert. He'd be in about twice, maybe three times a week. More for the quiet company than the reading. A glass of wine then he'd hit the horror section."

"Did he have a preference?"

"I asked him once. 'Anything but vampires,' he said."

"Did he come in or leave with anyone?"

"Not usually, but in the last month or so he'd sometimes sit next to this other man." Before Simon could ask, Kirst described him. "Tall, blond, blue eyes, pale skin, built like he could play football. The last few weeks they'd leave together. You don't think …"

"I try not to. It makes my head hurt. When was the last time this pale Viking was here?

"Come to think of it, the last time Robert was."

"What did he like to read?"

"Let me think. Mostly Westerns."

"Did he have a favorite?"

"Yeah, I think it was *Dark Night, Pale Rider.*"

Simon went to the small, Western section where he found the book. It was a battered paperback that had seen better days and many readers. He went back to Kirst.

"I'll take this. How much?"

"If you think it will help you find Robert's killer, it's yours. What do I tell the police if they show up?"

"The same thing you told me. But don't mention the book. It won't help them."

♟

The next afternoon, Timothy Payton picked Simon up outside Sebastian's.

"Always Sebastian's. Why is that? Do you live there?"

"Some floors above it. Why the ride?"

"The brass hats are getting worried. One of the cops on the scene used his phone to sneak a photo of Ballard, that's Robert's last name in case you didn't know."

"I didn't. I don't know David's either."

"Yeah, neither do we. It's like he doesn't exist. But he's a vampire, so I guess he doesn't. Anyway, like I was saying, one of the first cops on the scene took a picture of Ballard on the bed with the stake sticking out of him. The Crime Lab catches you doing that they seize the phone as evidence. So do we. So the first ones on the scenes get all the good shots. You expect it. You also expect them to keep it to themselves, no sharing, no posting. You don't expect them to sell the pics to the Star. The people who run that rag were kind enough to give us a heads-up about tomorrow's headline — "Vampire Murder in Harbor East." So the heat's on, and the last thing any of us need is to be seen talking to someone ..."

"Notorious?"

"I was going to say well-known but that will do. Not that they'd mention your name."

"They know not to do that."

"Yeah, especially after the last time. They'd say something like "A well-known expert in the occult has been called in.""

"So what you're saying is that you can't be seen with me."

"That, and the commissioner called the deputy who called the major who called my lieutenant who told me to wrap this thing up

ASAP. Please tell me you have something for me."

"Only a description of a suspect seen in the company of Robert Ballard shortly before he was killed. Just got it last night." Simon told Payne about Late Night Reads and the tall, blond man.

"Well, it's something. I'll send a sketch guy down there tonight. Maybe the Star will hold off another day if we promise them a picture of our suspect."

"One of them, at least."

"Yeah, but we're keeping the vampire to ourselves. Unless …" Simon watched Payne's face, saw his cop mind start to work. "You don't think this blond guy is one too."

"It's possible."

Simon noticed that Payne was driving randomly around the city. From 25th Street to I-83 up to Coldspring then down Falls Road. He thought about asking him to stop on the Avenue so he could visit London Books. There he could ask Ginny about any tall, blond customers who like Westerns. London Books wasn't open at night, so if he had come in, that would rule him out as a vampire. He then decided it was best not to involve her. Instead, he let Payne take Falls Road back to I-83.

"Tim?"

"Uh, oh, first names. This must be serious."

"It is. Let's assume the killer is a vampire, instead of someone who just thought Robert was."

"Okay, let's assume that."

"When you catch them, what are you going with them?"

"The usual, I gue… Oh shit, I see what you're getting at. Even if we could subdue it at night, charge it at night, and take it to Central Booking at night, we have to bring it out in the daylight at some point."

"At which point they boil away in front of the cameras unless it's cloudy or raining, and you can't count on that. And consider what you've already done."

"What's that?"

"You've allowed a vampire access to a building full of people that they consider a food source. People who can't escape."

"Wouldn't it control itself?"

"Vampires control themselves to avoid notice. This one will have already been noticed. They might even turn some of the prisoners out of anger or vengeance."

"Damn, so there's really only one thing to do."

"I'm afraid so."

"Then we better make damn sure we get it right."

They drove in silence for a while. Payne got off I-83 and took Fallsway to Lombard then to Light and into the Southern District.

"Do you have anything for me?" Simon asked Payne.

"Just the results of the autopsy. How did you know?"

"Know what?"

"That the stake went in post-mortem. According to the ME, Ballard's insides were a mess. Massive internal trauma. 'Like a truck hit him,' she said. The stake was just for show. A middle finger to this David."

Payne's a good detective, Simon thought. *Once he starts thinking, really thinking, he'll come to the obvious conclusion. I told Frederick that I could find Daivd when I needed to. I guess I need to.*

"Payne?"

"Yeah, Tombs?"

"Can you swing by Robert's apartment? There's something there I need."

"What?"

"A pair of pajamas."

"Should I ask why?"

"Please don't. If I'm right, we'll have this thing put to bed in a few days. No pun intended."

"That will be the day."

Later that afternoon, just as evening began to fall, Simon prepared for the night. He loaded a .32 semiautomatic pistol with a clip of cartridges containing silver bullets from Hi-Ho. Then he slipped a silver-bladed knife up his left sleeve and a spring-loaded device that fired a single wooden bolt up his right. An overlarge jacket covered the arsenal he hoped not to use. But he knew as well as Chekov that when weapons became part of the story they were likely to be used. Still, he hoped what was in his pocket would be all that he needed.

The Brewer's Hill section of southeast Baltimore was home mainly to newly married young professionals who found living in "the city" exciting. It had become so popular that any available open space, including alleys, was soon filled with condominiums and townhomes.

David's pillow led Simon to a midlevel condo in what had once been a Knights of Columbus meeting hall.

It was close enough to dawn that Simon was sure the vampire would be in. Having had no trouble with the building door, Simon knocked on David's.

There was a pause followed by, "Is that you, Simon?"

"Who else could find one who did not wish to be found?"

"Very well. Enter freely and of your will."

The door opened without Simon having to turn the knob. Simon entered carrying a package. David was standing in his living room, dressed in pajamas made from the soil of his native earth, which in his case was Carroll County, Maryland.

"How did you find me?"

In answer, Simon threw him the package. "Traced you through these. I knew wherever you were, you'd have your special sheets or pajamas. I thought you could use an extra pair of pajamas."

"Clever." David indicated the sofa. "Please, have a seat."

"Thank you, but I prefer to stand."

"It's like that, then."

"I'm afraid so."

The two men, the man and the vampire, stood squared off as if they were on the main street of an old Western town, the sun high, Colt .45s on their hips. But that was only in the kind of novels the blond man read. This was modern day, and the showdown was in an urban living room.

Simon was fast. The vampire was faster. Simon knew he'd had less time than a pitched ball reached the batter to react.

"Why are you here, Simon?"

"Robert was not killed by the stake. But you knew that when you thrust the stake into him."

"Robert was already dead. I knew the stake would confuse the issue and buy me time."

Maybe David relaxed. Maybe Simon did too. If so, it did not relieve the tension in the room.

"You arrived just after feeding. The police were pounding on your door. If they came in and found you, you knew there would be blood, all of it theirs. So you used the stake, grabbed the pajamas, and jumped off the balcony."

"I've fallen further and survived. And yes, I did all that but I didn't kill him."

"I know."

Only then did David relax. Simon waited for him to collapse on the sofa to relax as well. Still, he remained standing.

"How do you know?"

"If you had just killed someone you cared about you would not have hesitated to go through the police about whom you cared nothing."

"Unfortunately true."

"So what stopped you this time?"

"Innocent or not, killing police in your city would be a good way of getting staked and being put out in the sun to dry. Instead, I trusted you. But even so, why did you trust me?"

"The police arrived too soon. Your rival was waiting and watching. When you returned, he called the police. In that part of town, they respond fast. He knew you'd either fight or flee. Either way, you'd be hunted."

"And you'd be the hunter."

"Yes."

"So what happens next?"

"That part's easy. You die."

The next morning, Detective Timothy Payne met Simon Tombs behind David's condo building. Simon was standing by a pile of ashes and bits of charred bone he'd taken from his pocket and a wooden bolt from his wrist-mounted crossbow.

"So this is him?"

"This is what's left of David, former 'vampire king' of Baltimore."

"What happened"

"Off the record, let's say I found him through his personal effects. There was a confrontation just before dawn. I staked him, brought him down here, and waited for the sun to rise."

"And on the record?"

"No comment. Make up whatever story you want. Say he went crazy and thought his partner was a vampire. Consumed with guilt, he burned himself to death. To be honest, I don't really care. David was sort of a friend of mine and I did what needed to be done. The rest, detective, is up to you."

The next evening, at another of David's safe houses, Simon asked the now "dead' vampire, "Where will you go, because you can't stay in the city. I've already called Frederick. He'll be looking for a new Baltimore."

"I hear Talbot County is nice. It's unclaimed, lots of small towns, plenty of tourists, and a nice bookstore. But what about …?"

"Let me take care of him."

It took Simon two nights of searching but, using a battered paperback that had seen better days, he finally located the tall, pale-skinned blond man who had seduced Robert Ballard and so gained access to his and David's apartment. Simon imagined this man waiting just outside the front door until Robert said, "Well, come on in." Invitation enough for a vampire. Once inside, maybe he fed off Robert, maybe he didn't. That wasn't important. Killing him to implicate David was. It wasn't the most well thought-out plan but it had almost worked.

Simon found the blond vampire in an after-hours place similar to Bartleby's. Only this one was located in Violetville off Benson Avenue just behind St. Agnes Hospital. The man was sitting in the back booth, his back to the rear wall, the better to see who entered and left. Simon slid in next to him.

"Who the hell are you?"

"The name's Simon Tombs. I take it you're the new Baltimore."

"Yeah, what of it."

The silver-coated bolt hardly made a *pfft* sound as it left Simon's left sleeve and buried itself in the vampire's heart. Before the vampire could respond the silver began its work. Within minutes, the vampire who would have been Baltimore was a pile of dust. Simon left without being noticed. The dust eventually was wiped up and thrown away.

The Hours

The Hours was located in what had been St. Brighid's Abbey, a former monastery in the western mountains of Maryland. So close was it to the state line that it was said that if a strong man threw a stone from one of its balconies it would land in West Virginia. Built by a Celtic order of monks and later taken over by the Franciscan Brothers, it was now a secular retreat for those in need of meditation and reflection.

Simon Tombs was there at the suggestion of Molly Charm. Molly was married to Detective Terry Charm, a homicide detective with the Baltimore Police Department. She was also an angel. Simon knew this because her feet never quite touched the floor.

They met one day by accident, both of them having attended morning service at the Basilica of the Assumption on Cathedral Street. Neither left after the mass had ended.

"Checking in with the Boss?" Simon asked as he slid into her pew.

"No need. They know where I am. It's just, well, sometimes I'm just drawn here."

"Why are you here, Molly? And I don't just mean this church."

"Even angels need time off now and then. I came down about five years ago. Soon after that, I met Terry and when we fell in love I extended my vacation."

"You can do that?"

"Who understands love better than …" She pointed toward the altar and the large cross hanging over it. "I'll be with Terry until it's time for him to move on. Then I'll go back to work. What about you? Why are you here? And I do mean this church."

"Too much has been happening. I … just need some peace and quiet, some time to think. There have been too many demands lately. Too many people know who I am, or rather, who Simon

Tombs is. Maybe it's time to move on and become someone else."

That's when Molly told Simon about The Hours and its history. "It's a good place to go if you need time away from the world. They follow a Rule of sorts — work, chanting, secularized prayer, whatever that is, and time for solitude and meditation. No electronics are permitted, and the only time kept is the liturgical Hours, hence the name. If you can't find yourself there in a week or two, you are truly lost."

"Sounds like a good idea, maybe I'll give it a try."

Just then a bell rang from within the sanctuary. Simon looked at Molly and spocked an eyebrow.

"I already have mine, thank you very much," she said.

"So where are they?"

"If I don't show them to my husband, what makes you think I'm going to show them to you?"

"Said the actress to the bishop. Thanks for the advice, Molly. Now let me give you some. You should tell him, about the wings and all."

"I know, but I worry about how he'll take it."

"Molly, Charm helped me take down a demon from Hell. I think he can handle his wife being an angel."

"You're probably right. Marriage is all about trust, isn't it."

"I don't know about marriage, but love certainly is. I have to go. Say hi to Charm for me."

Three days later Simon was being shown to his room by Brother Thomas.

"Here it is, Simon. We used to call our rooms 'cells' but it made some people nervous, so room it is. The bathroom is in there. You'll find your robes in the wardrobe. You're required to wear them, although what you wear or don't wear underneath is up to you."

Thomas paused allowing Simon to smile in appreciation of

his joke. "As I'm sure Brother Joseph will have told you, dinner is at Vespers. That's …"

"I'm familiar with the Hours, Brother."

"Good. After dinner, the rest of the schedule will be explained and you will be given the opportunity to sign up for work details. That's it until dinner. May you have a peaceful stay."

"And peace to you as well, Brother."

With a "Thank you," Thomas left, closing the heavy, wooden door behind him. Simon found himself waiting for a thud or click that would indicate he was being locked in his room. Not hearing any, he decided that he'd been reading and watching too many horror novels and movies.

Going to the wardrobe, Simon saw a choice of habits — wool or cotton with a choice of colors — black, deep red, and brown. No white, which Brothers Thomas and Joseph had worn. Simon guessed that color was reserved for the staff. The nights tending to be chilly in the mountains, he chose brown wool. Deciding against going commando, he left his underwear on. Then he sat out on the balcony to contemplate nature and finish reading *Dark Night, Pale Rider*.

Dinner was a hot, thick stew, diner's choice of beef or vegetarian. While eating, Simon took the time to look over the company. Not counting himself, there were twelve at table, mostly guests, but a few of the staff. Their habits told him little else. Loose as they were, people's bodies were hidden. Simon supposed that was the point. And he didn't dare make guesses as to gender or age, even to himself. Except for a generalized prayer of thanksgiving at its start, the meal was eaten in silence.

There was common time afterward, the brothers and sisters introduced themselves, as did the guests. Beyond first names, no one seemed inclined to give much information about themselves.

As part of the "monastic experience," everyone was expected to work for the betterment of the community. Simon volunteered for library work — sorting, cataloging, and shelving books between the Hours of Terce and Sext (9 am and noon). He also agreed to tend Brighid's Fire between Matins (midnight) and Lauds (3 am). The way he'd been sleeping lately he'd be awake during those hours anyway. He might as well be of use. And it gave him his afternoons free.

"Before we go into the chapel for prayer, song, and group meditation," a monk called Brother Jerome said, "are there any questions?"

No one else had any so Simon asked his. "I noticed that part of the northside abuts a mountain. Does the monastery extend into it?"

"Yes, … Simon is it? There are caves. The founding monks, if that is what they were, appear to have originally lived in the caves and gradually built outwards. The caves go deep and now we use them for storage and natural wine cellars. We also maintain the ossuaries that were found there."

"What are ossuaries?" a guest named Dorothy asked.

Simon knew, but this wasn't his party and he let Brother Jerome answer. After all, if the monk hadn't wanted to talk about them he would not have mentioned them.

"An ossuary is something that serves as the final resting place for skeletal remains. In places where burial space is limited, such as here, the deceased are temporarily buried. Once they've decayed naturally, their remains are transferred to an ossuary. The founders used wooden chests, most of which have themselves decayed. The Franciscan Brothers who restored the monastery used chests made from stone in which to place the remains of their brethren. As you know, although we continue the monastic tradition, ours is a secular endeavor but we maintain the ossuaries out of respect."

"May we see them?"

As if expecting this question, Jerome smiled and said, "It's possible. As long as it is understood that the caves of the dead are sacred places and the proper respect is maintained. Now, it is time to go into the chapel. Tonight's services will be from the Buddhist tradition."

Terce came earlier than Simon expected, at least it felt like it. Brighid's Fire was outside on a western-facing patio. When he arrived, Sister Agatha was waiting for him.

"Right on time," she said, as the bells began to ring Matins.

Sister Agatha was a large woman. Her face was unlined but her grey hair put some age on her. Her voice was a bit raspy as if she had smoked heavily in the past. "The job is simple, really. Just throw wood on the fire when it looks like it might be getting low. Other than that, enjoy the night."

This said, Agatha did not show any signs of wanting to leave. So Simon took a seat on one side of the fire and Agatha on the other and they talked.

"Has it ever gone out?" Simon asked.

Agatha shook her head. "Not for the ten years I've been here. From what I've heard, it never has. It's said to have burned since the Celts who built this place first lit it in honor of St. Bridget, or maybe the goddess Brighid. Hell, maybe they're one and the same."

"Celts?"

"I think so, just from the name."

That makes sense, Simon thought. "What about when the founders left?"

"Let's see, that would have been just before the Civil War. As far as I know, the fire was kept burning. Maybe some of the Celts remained, or members of an indigenous nation kept it going."

"Either that or Brighid, however you spell her name, fed it."

"Whatever. From their journals, when the Franciscans arrived about ten years later, they found the fire burning. When our order bought the place from them, keeping it burning was part of the deal. Well, I'd best be going. Prime comes early. Brother Jonas will be here at Lauds to relieve you."

She got up to leave, then paused. "I suppose you noticed that the Order of the Hours, besides being pan-denominational, is also co-ed. And unlike the Franciscans, there's no vow of celibacy."

Her offer was plain. Simon smiled and said, "One of the reasons I'm here is for the solitude."

"I understand. Well, if you change your mind, just show up a bit before Matins. There's more than one way to keep a fire burning."

After Agatha left, Simon took her advice and enjoyed the night. *Good choice,* he told himself. *It beats gardening or wood chopping.* Stray thoughts intruded — vampires, haunted books and houses, Wine he did not dare drink, not yet anyway. He put them behind him, except that every so often Simon felt that he was in a story. Most times he was the protagonist, sometimes the antagonist. He'd been the watson, the helper, and sometimes just someone watching the action.

Am I in one now? he wondered. *It's the perfect place for it. A group of strangers in an isolated abbey high up in the mountains. A storm comes up, cutting the landline which is our only connection to the outside world. Then a shot in the dark, a scream in the night. Someone's murdered and we're all suspects except for the one person, that would be me, who tries to solve the case before there are more deaths. Which of course there will be.*

Or one of the guests is a spy, an agent of a united network for law enforcement. HOURS is an acronym for an organization out to, dare I think it, take over the world. The spy seeks my help and together we save the day, unfortunately destroying the monastery in the process.

And what about the bones of the dead? There were some interesting books in the library. Someone reads the wrong one aloud and the bones …

Stop it, Simon. Not everything is a story. Sometimes a vacation is just a vacation. Time for more wood on the fire, and then I'll step outside and, when the Moon shines, watch for snallygasters.

None of the above happened. One day ran into another as Simon fell into the routine of the monastery. The outside world began to fade and he almost forgot it still existed. He knew he'd have to go back but until then he'd just enjoy the quiet.

It was on Simon's sixth day at The Hours. Or possibly the seventh. Maybe it was the eighth. Rested, relaxed, and not yet thinking of returning to the real world, Simon had lost track of the days. Only the hours mattered.

"I guess that's why they named it what they did," he said out loud one morning between Matins and Lauds as he fed the fire.

"You're probably right."

Strange, I didn't hear anyone come in, Simon thought and looked around for the speaker.

He found him sitting on a bench near the outside doorway. He was a largish man of about fifty, wearing a brown habit, its cord tied in three knots in the Franciscan style. *He must have come in from outside*, he thought, then realized he had not seen him before, not in the chapel or during the meals. *Maybe he …*

The fire shifted, throwing its light on the man. That's when Simon saw that he was mostly transparent.

"So that's it," Simon remarked, more to himself than the stranger, "I'm in another ghost story."

"I'm afraid so." The man's accent was of a different century and maybe from Northern Virginia or Southern Maryland. "I'm very sorry to have interrupted your meditation, but would you kindly tell me what year this is?" Simon told him. "That long? Let's see. I think I died …" he shook his head … "I don't know the date. As I'm sure you've learned, here only the Hours matter. I seem to recall a war."

"Which one?"

There was ghostly laughter followed by "Ah, yes, a good question. There's always a war. I remember there were young men, and it's always young men who fight the wars, isn't it? These had come from a war in Europe. Most had been shot. Many had lost limbs. Some had horrible burns and others suffered from gas inhalation."

"The First World War, 1914-1918. The U.S. got involved in 1917."

"The *First* World War? You mean they were foolish enough to do it again. No, never mind, there are always fools. I'm Brother Michael. I'd offer my hand but you'd only be shaking air."

"Why the visit, Brother? No one mentioned the place was haunted."

"They don't know. Me and the others haven't made ourselves known. After all, we were always a solitary order and kept mostly to ourselves. As it was in life, so it is in death. I see them sometimes, listening to the chanting, saying the prayers, all of them waiting to be released from whatever binds them here."

"And what binds you here, brother? What are you waiting for?"

"Someone like you, Simon." Not at all surprised, Simon nodded. "You're different from any of the others who have come here. Here I am a ghost and you accepted me as if it was that Agatha woman who came in. There's a touch of the strange about you, Simon, and a little of the weird. Part of you is a trickster, and another has walked with the Divine. And, if I'm right, you've done more than walk with both angel and demon."

"I won't say you're wrong, brother," Simon answered with a smile. "Tell me, what do you need with someone like me?"

The ghost sighed, making a long and mournful noise which Simon felt in his soul. "Like you, I was, still am, different from most men, at least when it came to love and desire. I had the misfortune to grow up in a faith that taught that my wants and desires were sinful. I think most did back then. But that's not to say I didn't find men like myself, but the joy I gave and received was tainted by guilt. So I came here. I know, I know, why did someone who desired men seek refuge in a house full of them? The robes hide us, hide who we are. And as I'm sure you've found, you can lose yourself in the Rule, the Ritual, and the Hours. I found that I could, and for many years hid myself from myself."

"Excuse me, Brother, but Lauds may be close."

"A polite way of telling me to get to the point. Don't worry, there's time. In a place like this, there's always time. It was during the war I mentioned that I found you cannot hide forever. There was a young man, a corporal with an angel's face and hair to match. There was nothing physically wrong with him but every night and most of the day he relived the horror of that war. He'd scream until he wore himself out then collapse. When he woke, he was calm enough to eat, talk, and even pray a little. Then the demons of battle would find him again. St. Bridget's was the right place for him. Here the walls are thick and the rooms many. I was assigned to care for him. I fed him when he was hungry and watched over him as he slept. And when the terrors took him, I'd hold him until he calmed. How was I to know that he was a man like me? He made the first advance. And I responded. And this time there was no guilt to go with the joy."

"Were you caught?"

"No, nothing like that. The abbot and the prior were pleased that I was able to calm him. Of course, they didn't know how I did it. Three months we had. I think it was three. Soon he was well enough to eat with the others, as long as I was by his side. We would walk the grounds and even visit the chapel when it was empty. On seeing this, the prior decided that Benjamin, that was his name, Benjamin Chandler, was well enough to be released and returned to active duty. I was at Mass when the prior gave him the news. He told me later that Benjamin took it calmly. He got up from his chair and shook the prior's hand, asked him to thank me for all I had done, then, before he could be stopped, threw himself from his second-floor window."

Brother Michael fell quiet. He cupped his hands over his face as if mourning his lost love all over again. Finally, "They wanted to bury him as a suicide. I argued that his death was the result of an unsound mind and so no blame should be attached to him. The prior objected but the abbot agreed. Having no family, Benjamin was buried here. His bones were later disinterred and his ossuary placed in our crypt. I don't remember much after that. I must have had a stroke of some sort. I remember passing out and when I awoke, I was as you see me now."

"You were not to blame, Brother."

"I know that, Simon, but something keeps me here."

"I'll think about what it might be. I'm sure you have your own ideas but fresh eyes and all that. Come see me tomorrow after Lauds."

Michael fell silent, and Simon got the feeling that he wanted to proceed that night or rather, morning. But Simon was not inclined to take the word of a ghost who'd been dead for over a century. Maybe the cause was as he suspected, love that did not die with death, but he could not discount the possibility that something else bound Michael to this world.

There were footsteps, and the inner door opened. Bother Michael faded away. A dark-skinned man with grey hair stepped in. "It's Lauds, Simon. You're relieved."

"Thank you, Brother."

One nice thing about Simon's job in the library was that he had access to the monastery records. Brighid's Celts did not keep any, but the Franciscans more than made up for it. Every part of their monastic life was documented — expenses, earnings, donations, and bequests. The dates on which monks entered the order, their former and adopted names, dates of departure and death. Most importantly for Simon, the causes of death were listed along with the final arrangements — which bodies were returned to the families for burial, and which wound up in the ossuary crypt.

The library was not busy, and Simon worked mainly without supervision. It was a simple matter to find the records he needed. They were in a journal from just after the end of the war. The journal's pages were yellowed and loose, and written, presumably by the prior, in Latin in a crabbed hand. Simon had barely started when the bells tolled Sext. Fortunately, the voluminous robes everyone wore were good for more than hiding their bodies. They also served to conceal books removed from the library without permission.

Back in his room, Simon took his time reading his purloined book. (*It is for a good cause*, he assured himself, *and I'll return it tomorrow.*)

The prior's account of Chandler's death was much the same as Michael's, except that when the prior gave him the news, he did not react as calmly as Michael said he did.

When I told young Chandler that he would be returning to service, the prior wrote, *he grew quite disturbed. He shouted that he could not leave, could not abandon his beloved. In my innocence I thought he was speaking of Our Lord, but when I told him that he could worship Christ anywhere he cried out, "No, not God, it was He who put me here. No, it's Michael. He is my beloved and my lover." Chandler then proceeded to tell me in what ways he and Brother Michael were "lovers."*

I did not believe him, could not believe that one of our brethren would take advantage of a mentally unstable man and commit unnatural sins with him. When I told Chandler this, he became enraged and rushed me. I defended myself but in pushing him away I pushed too hard. Chandler stumbled back, went out the window, and fell to his death.

I failed Chandler. If nothing else, I should have had Brother Michael with me when I told him the news. If he had then made his accusations I could have judged their truth by the brother's reaction. When I later questioned Brother Michael, he swore by all that was holy that he had done nothing improper with Chandler. He suggested that perhaps his sickness went deeper than anyone had believed.

Brother Michael keeps my secret. We have agreed on a story that absolves me of blame and does not mention Chandler's accusation against him. So many sins. Let this page serve as my confession. May you who read this forgive me.

"You are forgiven, Prior," Simon said as he closed the journal. "Not that you need it so long after the fact. Or maybe you do. Maybe you could not be forgiven until someone read your confession. If so, *ego te absolve a peccatis tuis.* May you now rest in peace."

That night, the hours between Matins and Lauds dragged on. Brother Michael appeared just before Gregory relieved him. Michael faded and reappeared next to Simon in the hall.

"You are no doubt hoping that we will descend to the crypt where I will take Benjamin's bones from his ossuary and place them in yours. Then you two will be united and he will either join you in this life or you will join him in his."

The look on Michael's face told Simon that was exactly what he was hoping.

"That is not going to happen. Wherever Benjamin is, I will not disturb him." They walked for a few minutes then, "A long time ago. Michael, you made a choice, no, several choices, none of them good. No matter that Benjamin made the first move, you took advantage of a mentally ill patient. Your patient. Then you committed the sin of Peter when the prior questioned you. In covering up Benjamin's death, you caused the prior to lie as well. You're lucky that God is more Merciful than they are Just."

"Then what can I do? Tell me, please?"

"I have told you. He that hath ears to hear, let him hear. Now, don't bother me again."

A few days later, Simon returned to Baltimore, mostly renewed in spirit and ready for whatever challenges came his way, except for one matter. Which is why he called Molly and asked her to meet him at the Basilica.

He told her all that happened then in the quiet of the church asked, "You knew, didn't you?"

"How would I? I'm on vacation, remember? Still, the word angel does mean messenger."

"Then from you to me to Brother Michael, consider the message delivered. Do you think he'll figure it out?"

"That all he has to do is repent, ask forgiveness, and maybe weep a little? You gave him a good hint with the sin of Peter. And if he does, I have it on good, no, the best Authority that someone who has already forgiven him will be waiting."

There is No Time in Hell

The is no time in Hell, no day and no night. No one sleeps. To sleep is to dream. Pleasant dreams have no place in Hell and nightmares are everywhere.

Douglas Sorenson's nightmare was a large, black Hellhound. When alive, Douglas had been a hitman. Known as "Dog," he murdered people for his masters. Caught, convicted, and sentenced to die, Douglas repented and went to the electric chair knowing he'd have to pay for his sins, each and every one of them. The hound was his penance.

Douglas first saw the hound when he awoke in Hell. It was a shadow come to life with red eyes and sharp, white teeth. When it began to stalk him, Douglas did the only thing he could, he ran through the woods in which he'd found himself. Naked as he was, rocks and sticks cut deep into his feet. Branches slashed his face and sliced his chest, arms, and legs. The hound pursued him silently except for the crashing it made as it chased him.

Douglas ran until he thought he would collapse. Then he heard the hound getting closer and found the strength to run some more.

Is this it, he thought, *is this my penance? To run forever, hit and cut by every sharp and pointed thing in this damned forest and chased by a hound that wants to eat me? Maybe if I can just get out of these woods …*

He tripped. When he fell, his arm struck a large rock and broke, the pain of the fracture running through his body.

The hound came closer. Douglas got back on his feet and started running again, his every movement adding to the agony of his broken arm.

He did not see the hole. He fell again and this time twisted his ankle.

Maybe I'll just lay here and let the damned thing eat me. Will it be over then? Will that satisfy God and make up for the people I killed? Or do I have to get out of these woods?

Again he got to his feet. He tried to run but could only hobble forward.

The hound was still behind him, coming closer, closer, closer.

Then it wasn't. Nor was there any noise of pursuit.

Is that it? Is it over, Douglas wondered. He looked back. Nothing. He looked ahead and, in the distance, saw the brightness of a clearing.

Finally, he thought. Then he asked himself how long he'd been running. As there is no time in Hell, he couldn't say. He might have been running for ten minutes, ten years, or ten centuries. He decided that it didn't matter. It was over, all he had to do was limp to the clearing and it would be over.

The hound attacked suddenly, its large front paws knocking him to the ground. It straddled him and growled in his face, its fetid breath gagging Douglas. Had there been anything in his stomach it would have come up. As it was, the dry heaves he suffered hurt so badly that Douglas realized that the hound had probably broken most if not all of his ribs.

Then the hound smiled the way all dogs do when they have done something to please their masters. Douglas knew that smile, it reminded him of the pleasure he felt every time he pulled the trigger, the pleasure of a job well done, of having ... pleased his masters.

Before Douglas had time to contemplate this revelation, the hound jumped off his body and bit down on him, its sharp teeth cutting into his side, penetrating who knew how many organs. More pain was added to his twisted ankle and broken arm and ribs. With Douglas still trapped in its jaws, the hound threw him high into the air. When Douglas landed, every bone in his body shattered at once.

Douglas lay there, each broken bone adding its own pain to that which Douglas already felt.

"No more," he said to the hound. But this was Hell where the words "no more" had no meaning. And so the hound grabbed and threw him again, and again, and again until the bones in his body were dust and paste.

Playtime over, the hound was hungry. It started with Douglas's feet and worked upward, biting and chewing. Douglas screamed in agony as he was slowly eaten. Soon only his head was left. His cheeks went first, then his jaw, then his face. Finally, there was a crunch as the hound cracked and devoured his skull and slurped up his brain.

If Douglas thought that was the end he was wrong. His soul was immortal and could not die, so he was fully aware as he was digested and, worse, eliminated. Only when he was a foul-smelling pile of dog crap on the forest floor did Douglas lose consciousness.

But not for long. When Douglas again awoke naked in the woods the hound was there. When it began to stalk him, Douglas took to the woods wondering how long this chase would last and if it would end differently.

There is no time in Hell. Still, Douglas had his own way of keeping track. He knew how many people he had killed. He also knew how many he had injured or permanently disabled on the orders of his masters. Sometimes killing wasn't needed. It was often sufficient for someone to be violently made an example of as a warning to others. Adding them to the ones Douglas had murdered, the total number of his victims was 197.

He had worked that out after he had confessed to the priest and was awaiting execution. *Almost twenty a year*, he thought. *Call it an even two hundred. That's how many lives I have to pay for.*

Two hundred. An easy number to remember. There was another number. That was the number of times he'd been chased, caught, tortured, eaten, and shat out. Each time was as bad as the first. The woods did not grow less friendly. Instead, they changed every time. There were the snares — trees would fall, trapping him beneath them. Easy prey for the hound. Several times he'd fallen into a disguised pit. The hound would watch him from above, sometimes befouling him with its waste, then jump down to finish him. Once, with Douglas lying in a deep pit, his body in agony from the bones he'd broken in his fall, the hound had simply left, allowing Douglas to suffer until it deigned to return to finish the job.

Douglas endured all this and worse, knowing that each torturous pursuit brought him closer to the number of his victims, the number of his release. After all, that was the deal he had made with God through the priest. He'd pay for each and every one of those he'd hurt or killed. Then he'd be free of the Pit and paroled into Paradise.

Poor fool. Poor damned fool, to believe that it would be that easy.

Douglas's hound, like all of its kind, was not a fallen demon. Nor was it a damned soul, condemned to eat human flesh for the many sins it had committed. No, the hounds were creatures of the Pit, created for a specific purpose. They normally roamed the vast reaches of Hell, searching for the Fallen and the Damned. Once they found their prey, they'd devour it, sending it to the lowest reaches where its suffering would begin anew. Their only restraint was that they were not to torment souls that shone with an inner light, although they were allowed to chase them in a certain direction, causing any demons who might torment them to pause, for it is not wise to get between a hound and its prey.

So it was that Douglas's hound was confused, as much as it could be. Never before had it been commanded to chase and eat a particular soul over and over again. But it was a good hound, always willing to do its Masters' bidding.

There was something else. The Hounds of Hell were the stuff

of shadows, having no substance of their own. And the souls they devoured were mostly shadows like themselves. While some of the essence of those souls remained with them, their meals were so many and so varied that none left an impression.

Douglas was different. Each time the hound devoured and shat him out, a little of him remained with it. Soon it began to understand him, to somehow know how the man, *its man*, thought. It knew how he would move and in which direction he would run. It knew when Douglas would run straight, when he would weave and dodge, and where he would hide and when. The hound was becoming one with its prey, and that made the game more interesting.

For, to the hound, it was a game, one it enjoyed. It did not know that, except for a winged almost-demon with a fiery sword who guarded a bridge, it and the other hounds were the only ones who found enjoyment in what they did.

The hound did not know how long it had played its game with the man but each time it played, the hound grew a little more aware. That came from repeated feedings each one of which left still more of the man inside it. The hound knew the man's name was "Douglas." It later learned that sometimes Douglas was "Dog" and that a hound was a kind of dog. So was it a dog as well? If so, was Douglas a sort of hound?

This is what confused the hound. As a creature of shadow, hunger, and instinct, it had not been made to think and wonder. That came from too much Douglas in its diet.

It had been played many games with Douglas and always they had been "chase, catch, play, eat, eliminate, and wait for Douglas to reform." But once the steamy pile of stink grew back into Douglas, the man would say a number. Each time the number was different. But it was not part of the game and so it didn't matter to the hound.

This time was different. Douglas said, "197" but did not run into the woods for the hound to chase him. Instead, he stood there and said, "This is ridiculous. Come on, dog, just eat me. It's time to get this over with."

Dog. Douglas had called it "dog." *He is dog*, its awakening mind thought. *And I am dog. We are one. He is my dog and I am his. But why isn't he playing the game?*

The hound stood there, waiting for Douglas to run and start the game. Douglas stood there waiting for the hound to attack. Neither moved. Finally, Douglas said,

"I get it. The chase and all that goes with it is part of it. Okay, girl, let's do it. I'll run and you chase. Let's see how long I can deprive you of your meal this time." He ran into the woods.

"Girl." Douglas called me "Girl." From that part of Douglas that was inside it, the hound knew what a girl was, and how it differed from a boy, which is what Douglas was. It accepted the designation and the name. *I am a girl*, she thought, *and I am Girl, for that is what Douglas named me.*

Then she took off after him.

A few games later, Girl sensed Douglas's excitement as another chase began.

"Come on, Girl. One last time," he said.

What did Douglas mean by "one last time?" Girl asked herself, knowing full well that there was no "last time" in Hell. As he ran off into the woods, she gave pursuit.

The game was different now. Douglas was a skilled runner and seldom stumbled or fell. His body was still cut by rocks, stones, branches, and the like, but he hadn't fallen into a hole for many chases now. It took longer and longer for Girl to catch him but that may have been because she enjoyed the game so much that she deliberately prolonged it. When she did catch him, she went for a quick kill.

There is no time in Hell but the chase seemed to go on forever yet was over too quickly. When Douglas reformed there was a smile on his face.

No one smiles in Hell, Girl thought. At least, she had never seen one.

"Thank you, Girl. You literally put me through Hell but it was worth it. I really could not have done it without you."

What is Douglas talking about? And why isn't he running?

"Any minute now." Douglas looked up into the dark, grey clouds that covered Hell. "Come on, take me. Ascend me or however these things work." Whatever Douglas was expecting didn't happen. "Come on, damn it. We had a deal. I confess and say I'm sorry. I get sent here and the dog eats me. We do this over and over until I make up for every person I killed or hurt. WHY AM I STILL HERE?"

Girl had eaten Douglas enough to know what a deal was. Having been created in the Pit she knew something else.

There are no deals in Hell.

Douglas started and turned toward Girl. "I heard that, in my head. What did you say? And since when do you talk?"

Since now, Douglas. I do not know how long I have been here. I do not know why I am supposed to chase and eat you. I do not know how long we have played this game. But I do know that deals made by Hell or in Hell do not count.

"No, this wasn't made here. It was made before I died. It was made by …" He found that he could not say the Name, not in Hell. "…By That Which Is Not Hell."

Girl knew what Douglas was talking about. She had sensed this "Not Hell" when she chased the Souls of Light.

Then maybe the deal is not yet complete.

Douglas shook his head. "No, I accounted for every one of them, from Shelly Green to Annette McKay and all those in between. All of them, everyone I hurt."

Douglas thought of Annette McKay. She was the last person he killed. She was the reason he had been arrested. She was the reason he had been executed. She was one of the ones he had regretted killing.

Poor woman, he thought. *So much to live for. A young woman with a husband and child and I took her away from them.*

I took her away … from them. And that must have hurt … them. So I hurt … them. And how many more? How many more did I hurt by killing their loved ones?

As if it was waiting for Douglas to ask this question, the answer suddenly appeared in his mind. The name of each person who had mourned one of Douglas's victims, each person who had suffered because of someone he had killed or injured, and each person whom he had hurt by his actions came into his mind. There were hundreds, thousands of them. And their suffering had caused more suffering. And this suffering …

It was too much for Douglas. He fell to his knees and screamed in pain. Not the physical pain he had felt during the two hundred times Girl had chased and eaten him, but a pain that cut into his soul.

And he felt real sorrow. Not the sorrow he felt before he died. Then, he was sorry for his sins because he feared punishment so he confessed, hoping to plea bargain his way into Heaven. Now, he felt the sorrow that comes with truly regretting all one has done.

And only with this repentance was he able to say the Name which had been denied him. Standing, he lifted his head and looked up into and past the dark clouds and shouted, "Oh my God, I am sorry for all I've done."

Then Douglas Sorenson collapsed and wept for all those he had hurt.

Girl was not sure what was going on but she had been a dog long enough that she knew what to do. Lying next to Douglas, she covered him with her great body and comforted him with her presence.

It is not possible to say how long they lay there. After all, there is no time in Hell. But Douglas eventually stopped crying. Carefully removing himself from Girl's embrace, he stood. Accepting his fate as right and just, he said, "Let's go, Girl. I've got a lot of harm to make up for."

Girl stood and shook herself the way all dogs have since they were created. When she saw him ready to be chased and eaten, she realized that she could do one but not the other, for the glow that shone from Douglas marked him as one of the Souls of Light and she could not harm them and could only chase them in one direction.

Or, maybe lead them. With her mouth, she gently took Douglas by the hand and led him out of the woods.

"Where are you taking me?'

I am not sure. We will know when we get there.

"And when will that be?"

It does not matter. There is no time in Hell.

The Way to Paradise

Is it me, Fel, Guardian Demon of the Bridge, asked herself, *or are there more of them than usual?*

By "them" Fel meant the demons who lingered near the Bridge just out of her reach, but not out of her sight. They were there in the hope that her attention would lapse and they could sneak past her into Heaven. Of course, they would be forcibly rejected but for one brief moment they would know the Joy they had forsaken long ago. And that was worth all the pain they would suffer on their return.

Or they were there in case she strayed from the boundaries set for her. This far and no further was the rule and should she take one step beyond that which was permitted, she'd be subject to the rule of Hell.

Then there were the rare Souls of Light, ones who had truly repented their sins and now sought Paradise. To gain it, they had to get close enough to the Bridge for Fel to protect them. If caught and destroyed before this, they had to start their journey over again.

There are more, Fel decided. *No matter, let them come. Maybe being this close to Salvation eases their pain. I was once one of them. I know how they feel. But if they come too far, they will feel the pain of a fiery sword.*

She looked at them and when her bright, blue eyes met their red ones they drew back.

They are no real threat, she thought.

In this, Fel was wrong.

Simon Tombs had spent most of the day dealing with the

executor of the Beatrice Newman estate. They had met to discuss Simon's purchase of Madison Collectibles, an antique shop Newman had owned at the time of her death. Simon already owned a haunted house; the last thing he needed was to own a formerly haunted museum but he reasoned that it was safer in his hands than anyone else's.

Now all I need is someone to run it for me. I wonder if Judas … no, he's not the kind to settle down.

When his phone rang he thought it was the executor formally accepting his offer. Instead, the caller ID read, "Detective Charm."

Mmmm, I wonder if Molly would consider taking it on. After all, who better than an angel on leave from Heaven? With this in mind, he thumbed the phone to answer.

"Charm, I was just thinking of you. There's no trouble I hope?"

"Tombs, we need, that is, Molly and me need to see you."

Not BPD work then. Otherwise, we'd be meeting at a diner. "I'll be right there."

Charm had sounded serious. Serious enough that Simon wondered if he should take one or more weapons. *No, he decided, one does go armed when visiting friends, unless said friends might be planning to kill you.*

He was at the Charm home on Arabia Avenue in forty minutes, having made good time driving against after-work traffic. The detective opened the door before Simon had a chance to knock. He was greeted with, "Why didn't you tell me my wife is an angel?"

Charm seemed disturbed about something but not about Simon's knowing Molly's true nature.

"It was not my secret to tell. I hope everything's okay with that."

Charm flashed a quick smile. "Everything's great. Ever been hugged by wings?"

"A few times," Simon said, remembering Fel and Nika. *And probably never again*, he said to himself.

His face serious again, Charm said, "Come on in. They're in the living room."

"They" were Molly (as expected) and Detective Sergeant Caitlin Hood. Molly was sitting on the couch. Charm joined her there. Caitlin was standing against the back wall, as far into the corner as she could be. Dressed in all black, she seemed to blend in with the shadows.

Appropriate, Simon thought, *she does know what evil, and good, lurks in the hearts of men. Of course, her being here means there's real trouble. I hope it's not me.*

Before he could start considering escape routes, Molly said, "Sit down, Simon." Her voice was gentle and compelling and before he could think about it, Simon felt himself sitting in a chair across from Charm and Molly. "What do you know about Fel?"

Simon felt a small bit of hope well up in his chest. But this did not seem like a celebration and so he tamped it down.

"The last I was told was that she had a purpose and was content."

"There is a bridge over the chasm between Paradise and the Pit. Being neither angel nor demon, Fel guards this bridge, keeping demons from crossing and allowing passage to repentant souls."

My bridge? Simon wondered. *No, the one I created was not between Paradise and the Pit but between Hell and Earth, specifically my apartment. It was the one the demons used to attack me. Fel destroyed it after she saved me. No, when she chose to save me. And where she is now is the price of her choice.*

"She's there because of me."

"No," Molly replied firmly. "She's there because she rebelled. That is her penance. And all has gone well, until now. The Fallen are massing against her, keeping repentant souls from reaching salvation. They will eventually attack the Bridge, seeking to overwhelm her and force their way across. There will be war with Fel as the first casualty."

Simon thought about this for a moment. "What happens when an angel dies?"

"Fel is not yet an angel."

"Then what happens when a demon dies?"

"Nothing good. But Fel is not quite a demon. She is unique. So who knows what might happen if she falls."

God knows, Simon thought, *but They work in mysterious ways.* And "God Knows" was also his answer to how Molly knew. After all, she worked for Them, even if she was on vacation.

Already knowing the answer, Simon asked,

"Molly, why are you telling me this?"

"As I told you once, Simon Tombs, the word angel means messenger."

"And as I replied the last time, 'Consider the message delivered.' Now, if you'll excuse me, I have something I have to do."

Returning to his apartment, Simon went out on his balcony, sat down, and looked up at the night sky, specifically the sky above the Starry Night hotel. Framed as it was by the taller buildings on each side of it, Simon had always thought of it as his own little window into Heaven. Usually he just relaxed and enjoyed the view. That night was different.

"I'm not going to ask why Fel?" he said to the Divine. "I'm sure You have Your reasons. Maybe it's as Molly said, Fel's unique and the only one who can do the job. I don't understand it but I get it. Mysterious ways and all that.

"We all know that I'm not going to ask for this cup to pass from me. I *am* going after her. Why else tell me? Getting into Hell isn't a problem. Enough people have told me to go there I certainly know the way. It's just that … for once in my many lives I'm not sure what to do when I get there. I mean, I'll be facing the hordes of Hell, some of whom don't like me very much. I'll be alone, unarmed, unprotect…"

Simon paused and thought about what he had just said. Something about a cup. Leaving the balcony, he walked over to the living room bookcase. There, on the top shelf, were two bottles of a very special wine flanked by a pair of chalice-like goblets.

"Very clever. Very clever indeed. Did You set this up ahead of time or are You just taking advantage of the circumstances? Well, if this isn't the special occasion I've been saving this Wine for, it will do until something bigger comes along."

The front door opened. Part of him hoped it would be Fel with a smile on her face and "April Fool" on her lips. Instead, it was Caitlin Hood.

She had changed and was now dressed in her BPD street uniform — department blue shirt and cargo pants, exterior flak vest which displayed her badge, and her duty belt on which was her service pistol, pepper spray, and baton. She held a shotgun in her left hand.

"So, when do we go to Hell?" she asked.

It is right that she is here, Simon thought just as Caitlin said, "I loved Fel too."

"I still love her, and I'd be honored to have you by my side."

"So, what's the plan?"

"First, go into the kitchen and get the big travel mug from the side cabinet." She did and when she returned Simon was sitting on his living room couch, a bottle of wine and two goblets on the small table in front of him.

"What is this, Simon?"

"Caitlin, have you ever heard of the Wedding Feast of Cana?"

She had but he told her the whole story, including how the last of the Wine of Cana wound up in his possession.

"So this is the wine Christ made from water?"

"Yes, and it's the best chance we've got." He opened the bottle and poured. "Now drink up."

"Wait, what's the travel mug for?"

"Not what, but who?"

"Oh, I see."

They drank, and having drunk, felt a warmth they had never known before.

"Now," Simon said, filling the travel mug with the Wine. "put this in one of your cargo pockets and let's go to Hell."

"Aren't you taking any weapons?"

"A knife up my sleeve and one strapped to my leg but I don't think I'll need them. After all, I'm Simon Tombs."

"Pride goes before the Fall."

"It's not Pride, but Confidence."

"Confidence is a good thing. Confidence and a .40 caliber is another. Here, I brought a spare." Caitlin handed Simon a pistol which he accepted and secured.

"Loaded with silver bullets?"

"Can't hurt."

"No, they can't. Now then, Caitlin my dear, I've been wanting to say this for a long time."

"Say what?"

"Hold me close."

When she did Simon said, "Think of Fel and your connection to her. Think of your feelings for her and that one night you two spent together. Now, imagine this connection as a thread connecting the two of you. Good, now let the thread become a cord, and the cord become a rope, and the rope become a bridge."

As Simon guided Caitlin he thought, *This better work. It has to. If I build a bridge, they'll know it. So it has to be Caitlin.*

"Do you have the bridge between you and Fel? Can you feel it? Can you feel her?"

"Yes, it's as if I could reach out and touch her soul."

"Then do it. Leave your mortal self behind and let's cross the bridge."

And she did. And Simon followed. And their souls were in Hell.

✦

The number of demons was growing, had been growing for, well, Fel could not say, maybe a day, maybe a century, maybe forever. But their number was growing. What would she do if they moved to overwhelm her? What *could* she do? Take one step onto the Bridge and fight them one by one. Never tiring, fighting forever or until they stopped. She'd enjoy that. But what of the Souls of Light? Already there was almost no path for them to take to the Bridge. Should any of them make it, she'd have to step aside to let them pass. Then the demons would rush her and them.

There was one final option. She had not been told this but she somehow knew it. While not quite an angel, she was still a creature of the Light and she would use her light if all seemed lost.

The number of demons seemingly doubled, then doubled again. The pathways for the Souls of Light were gone and Fel was being pressed. Her sword of light cut down demon after demon but still they came. She now had one foot on the Bridge. More fighting, more demons falling. Some fell into the Great Chasm where they would burn until they struck bottom and then suffer even greater pain. Others fell at her feet, piling up. Soon their fellows would be able to climb over them to get to her. She would be lost as would the Souls of Light. Only one thing to do —fly high and shine brightly until her light burned out. After that, she would have to put her trust in the Ones who sent her.

"Oh Lord," Fel shouted out, "into Your Hands I commend my spirit."

Before she could take flight, there was the sound of thunder and everything stopped — except for a man with an enormous debt to pay and a hound named Girl.

Caitlin's bridge led Simon and her across a seemingly endless chasm to a spot not too far from the bridge Fel was defending. On seeing her, his soul filled with love. Hell was a place that sorely lacked love so he held on to the feeling and made it part of his armor.

"Why is no one paying any attention to us?" Caitlin asked.

"Because they're focused on Fel. They're too involved in crowding her, hoping to force her further back on the Bridge or draw her away from it. She's holding her own but I'm not sure for how long. And from the looks of things, neither is she."

Simon saw demons fall at Fel's feet, piling up so others could climb over them. He knew Fel enough to sense that she was about to do something desperate.

Drawing the pistol he didn't think he'd need, he smirked and said, "Let's introduce ourselves, shall we."

Caitlin brought up her shotgun. They fired as one.

Thunder echoed throughout Hell and everything stopped.

Half the hellish horde kept their attention on Fel. The other half turned toward them. When they did, Simon smiled.

"Now that we have your attention, will you all please step aside? We have business with the lady at the bridge." He started moving toward them.

"Simon, are you sure this is a good idea?"

"It's the only one I have, but yes, I believe it is."

"Why?"

"Because, my dear sergeant, we drank the Wine and are now filled with the holy spirits."

Confident in his faith, Simon walked into the crowd of demons, which unwillingly parted to let them pass. None wished to come into contact with them due to the protective warmth of the Wine of Cana. Even the ones crowding Fel had to move aside. Soon he was standing next to the not-quite-a-demon and not-yet-an-angel of his dreams. (And what dreams they had been. Even in Hell, he was ashamed to think of some of them.)

"Simon!" Fel shouted. A smile was on her face but she kept her eyes on the foes amassed against them.

Simon knew what she was feeling for he felt it too. The lovers' need to embrace, to kiss, to do those things that would show both Paradise and the Pit what true love was and set the bar for lovers everywhere. Instead,

"Good to see you, Fel."

"Same here, Simon."

A demon dared to move too close to them. More thunder as

Caitlin blew off what passed for its head. None of the others dared move.

Good, Simon thought, *the Wine holds them back.* To Fel he said,

"You seem a little busy."

"Somewhat."

"You look like you could use a drink. Caitlin!"

Without taking her eyes off the demon horde, Caitlin took the travel mug from a cargo pocket and threw it toward Simon, who caught it and offered it to Fel.

"A Pepper Special?"

"Something a little stronger."

Trusting her lover, Fel took the mug and drank. Almost immediately the Wine of Cana began its work. Her demon self slowly faded as the Warmth of Paradise filled her being.

Fel turned and looked at the crowd. The demons backed away. When she moved toward them, they moved back even further as each step she took extended Heaven's realm.

"Best not go too far," Simon suggested.

Fel resumed her place at the Bridge. "Yes, you're right."

"Stay right there if you would," Simon said, "it's time for me to show off."

Stepping forward, Simon addressed the assembled demons.

"My name is Simon Tombs. As for you, you're nothing but nameless slaves who were proud and foolish enough to believe there was a better world outside of Heaven. This, as you know, was a lie but you believed it, made your Choice, and wound up here. I don't care about you. Your leaders, Hell's "inner circle," don't care about you either. Why else would they have you destroy the one chance you have to return to Paradise? But I'll let you find the answer to that riddle yourselves. Right now I want to talk to your masters, who I am sure are listening.

"Listen to me, oh Masters of Nothing. As I have told you before, I have read the First Book, the book on which was carved your true names, the names that Heaven gave you, the names by which you are known to the Divine. I know these names and unless you remove your army from this place, I will start calling them out so that your army will hear them. And what do you think they will do? They will use these names to seize your power for their own."

Simon paused for a response. When it didn't come, he shouted, "Well, I'm waiting, or do I have to start reciting?"

Slowly the demons departed, until there were none left. Only then did the lovers dare embrace, Fel enveloping Simon in her wings as they did so. How long they kissed none can say, for there is no time in Hell. Slowly, reluctantly they parted.

"It is not over," said a voice that was almost a whisper. Simon knew that voice, knew it belonged to one of the masters of the Pit. "You and your whores have won this time, Simon Tombs, but the Bridge remains. One day, we will find a way across."

"And I will be here to stop you," Fel replied. "every time you try. You will fail. You will always fail, for that is what Hell is. Now begone."

"What she said," Simon added. Then he said a name, a name that no human except Simon Tombs, who had not been fully human for many decades, could pronounce. The Pit master screamed as loudly as a whisper could, then exploded in a rain of red and black.

"That was to show that I wasn't bluffing," Simon said to whoever else was listening. To Caitlin and Fel he said, "I would not have done that if he had not called you whores."

"Is it true," Caitlin asked, "that you're staying to guard the Bridge? I thought, I mean, you drank the Wine."

"Yes. I did. It changed me, and I am forgiven. I could walk across the Bridge right now and be accepted into Heaven, but that would leave the Bridge unguarded and that I cannot do. Not until someone is willing to take my place."

Simon started to speak. Fel interrupted him.

"And it cannot be you, Simon. Or you, Caitlin."

"How about us, then?"

The three turned at the sound of the voice. Walking towards them was a man, one of the redeemed Souls of Light. Beside him walked a large, shadow-black dog that Simon and Fel knew to be a hound of Hell. The man was dressed in a suit that had been in style in the late 50s and early 60s. He came close and when he stopped, the hound sat at his side.

"My name," the man said, "was Douglas Serrano. Now it's Dog. When I was alive, I was a killer for the Outfit. I was caught and executed for my crimes. Girl here was first my tormenter and, now that I've repented, my partner and friend. I …" A low growl from Girl. "… that is, we will take your place at the Bridge."

"You've been forgiven," Fel said. "Your soul is bright with Their Light. Why not cross over?"

Dog sighed. "Because Girl is a creature of Hell and I'm not sure she would be welcomed in Paradise. And I will not abandon my friend. I'm sure you can understand that."

As one, both Simon and Fel said, "We can." Thinking of Barbara, Caitlin echoed, "So can I."

"But that's not the only reason. Before I died, I made a deal with God that I would pay for every person that I killed or made suffer. It turns out that there's a lot more of them than I thought. Forgiven or not, I've never gone back on my word and I'm not about to here. Guarding the Bridge will be my way of working off my debt."

"Are you sure?"

"Yes, ma'am, I am. Besides, it beats being eaten."

Before Dog could explain, there came a voice that this time was a shout rather than a whisper.

"Fools," the shadow said, "what makes you think we will permit this? We will blockade the Bridge as we just did so that no Soul of Light will reach you."

"Girl, you want to take this?"

Without standing, Girl let out a howl that was heard throughout the Pit. It was answered by every hound in Hell. On hearing this, a chill ran through all those present.

"These hounds might be creatures of Hell, but they are not Fallen or Damned. Attack one and you attack them all. Do you really want to face a pack of hounds that can rend your souls?"

When the shadow did not answer, Dog turned to Caitlin. "Pardon me for asking, Officer, but may I borrow your shotgun?"

Caitlin handed it over. "Keep it. I can get another one."

"Thank you." As soon as Dog had the gun he fired it at the shadow which blew apart as nicely as the first one did. He then walked over to Fel.

"Fel, Angel of Heaven, I relieve you." He stepped aside. "You may now enter Paradise."

At first, Fel did not cross. Instead, she looked at Simon.

Now I know how Rick Blaine felt, he thought before saying "Go," he said. "I will miss you and will always love you but your place is there," he pointed across the Bridge, "and nowhere else."

Fel smiled. "I will miss you and always love you, Simon Tombs. Thank you for everything."

With that, Fel spread her wings and set forth over the Bridge. Soon she was out of sight.

After Fel had gone to her much-deserved reward, Caitlin said to Simon, "Race you to my bridge."

"You can't," Dog said. "It's not there anymore. Girl and I watched it disappear as soon as you stepped off."

"So how do we get home?" Caitlin asked.

Simon smiled. There was the pentagram he had left behind in a storage facility in Frederick. That was too risky and too far from home. Besides, he didn't think they'd need it.

Looking up into the dark cloudy skies of Hell, Simon imagined another view, that of the sky above the Starry Night.

"Caitlin, once again I ask that you hold me tight." Once she did, he said to the sky that was in his mind, "The job is done. The bad guys have been foiled, the Bridge is safe, and Your lost sheep has been returned. Please, we would like to go home now."

And so they did, still in the embrace they were in when they left. Impulsively, they kissed, but only in friendship and in memory of Fel. Once they parted, Simon looked at the clock and noted that hardly any time had passed.

The spirits have done it all in one night, he thought. Then he heard Caitlin say, "I should go home and hug Barbara. Will you call Molly or should I?"

"I have a feeling she already knows. But I'll call her tomorrow. She'll want details. For now, I think I'll just sit out on the balcony and look past the stars and all the way to Paradise."

Biography

JOHN L. FRENCH is a retired crime scene supervisor with forty years' experience. He has seen more than his share of murders, shootings, and serious assaults. As a break from the realities of his job, he started writing science fiction, pulp, horror, fantasy, and, of course, crime fiction.

John's first story "Past Sins" was published in Hardboiled Magazine and was cited as one of the best Hardboiled stories of 1993. More crime fiction followed, appearing in Alfred Hitchcock's Mystery Magazine, the Fading Shadows magazines, and in collections by Barnes and Noble. Association with writers like James Chambers and the late, great C.J. Henderson led him to try horror fiction and to a still growing fascination with zombies and other undead things. His first horror story "The Right Solution" appeared in Marietta Publishing's *Lin Carter's Anton Zarnak*. Other horror stories followed in anthologies such as *The Dead Walk* and *Dark Furies*, both published by Die Monster Die Books. It was in *Dark Furies* that his character Bianca Jones made her literary debut in "21 Doors," a story based on an old Baltimore legend and a creepy game his daughter used to play with her friends.

John's first book was *The Devil of Harbor City*, a novel done in the old pulp style. *Past Sins* and *Here There Be Monsters* followed. John was also the consulting editor for Chelsea House's *Criminal Investigation* series. His other books include *The Assassins' Ball* (written with Patrick Thomas), *Souls on Fire*, *The Nightmare Strikes*, *Monsters Among Us*, *The Last Redhead, the Magic of Simon Tombs*, *The Santa Heist* (written with Patrick Thomas), *In the Ruins of Caerleon*, *Daylight Comes*, and *The Wages of Syn*. John is the editor of *To Hell in a Fast Car*, *Mermaids 13*, C. J. Henderson's *Challenge of the Unknown*, *Camelot 13* (with Patrick Thomas), *With Great Power ...* (with Greg Schauer) and (with Danielle Ackley-McPhail) *Devilish and Devine* and *Grease Monkeys*.

You can find John on Facebook or you can email him at jfrenchfam@ aol.com.

From the Author of the Murphy's Law series @ Deuz Cthulhu
MYSTIC INVESTIGATORS
BY
PATRICK THOMAS

A MYSTIC INVESTIGATORS OMNI
SHADOWS & BRIMSTONE
From the authors of
PATRICK THOMAS
& JOHN L. FRENCH

A MYSTIC INVESTIGATORS BOOK
MEAN STREETS
From the Author of Fairy With A Gun and Lore & Dysorder
PATRICK THOMAS

A MYSTIC INVESTIGATORS OMNI
ONCE UPON IN CRIME
From the Creators of the Wildside Chronicles
PATRICK THOMAS
& DIANE RAETZ

DOWN THESE
MEAN STREETS
of Magic & Monsters walk the
MYSTIC INVESTIGATORS

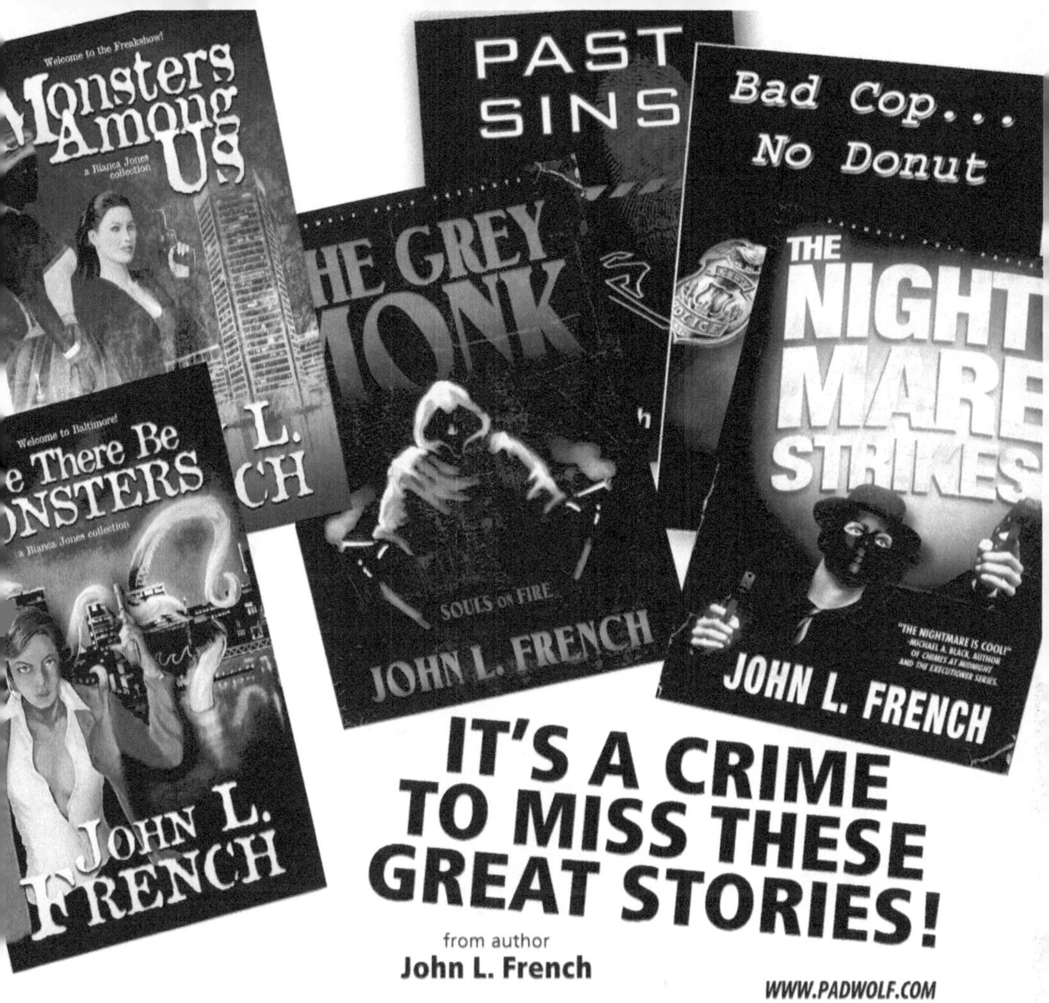

Welcome to the Freakshow!
Monsters Among Us
a Bianca Jones collection

PAST SINS

Bad Cop... No Donut

HE GREY MONK
SOULS ON FIRE
JOHN L. FRENCH

THE NIGHT MARE STRIKES
"THE NIGHTMARE IS COOL!"
-MICHAEL A. BLACK, AUTHOR
AND THE EXECUTIONER SERIES.
JOHN L. FRENCH

Welcome to Baltimore!
e There Be ONSTERS
a Bianca Jones collection
JOHN L. FRENCH

IT'S A CRIME TO MISS THESE GREAT STORIES!
from author
John L. French
WWW.PADWOLF.COM

You can't get better than 13!

APOCALYPSE 13
DEFCON 1

MERMAIDS 13
TALES FROM THE SEA

Camelot 13
Celebrating the spirit of Arthur and His Knights

LUCK 13
EDITED BY EDWARD J. MCFADDEN
Thirteen Tales of Crime & Mayhem
John L. French and Patrick Thomas

FUTURES

BIKINI JONES

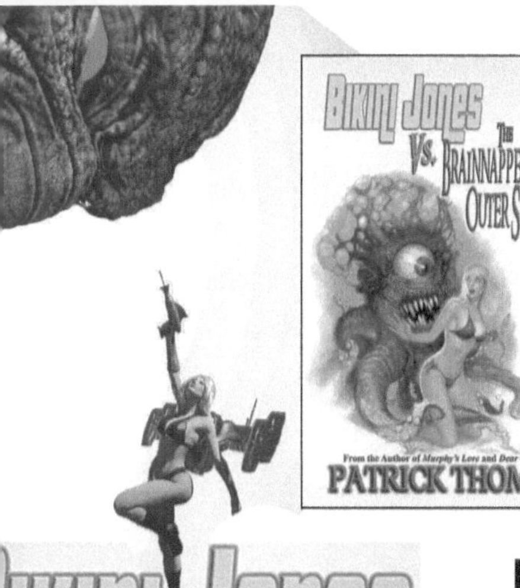

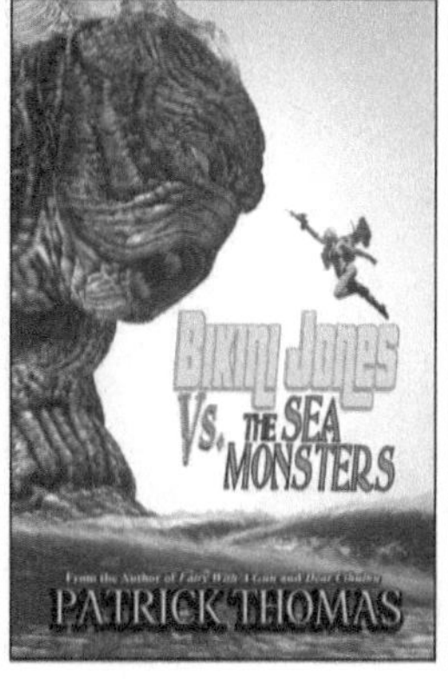

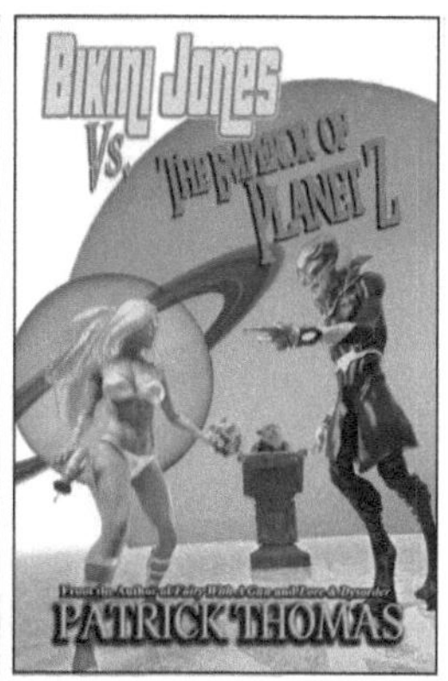

Being *CURSED* to wear a bikini
Won't stop this Hero
From *SAVING* the world

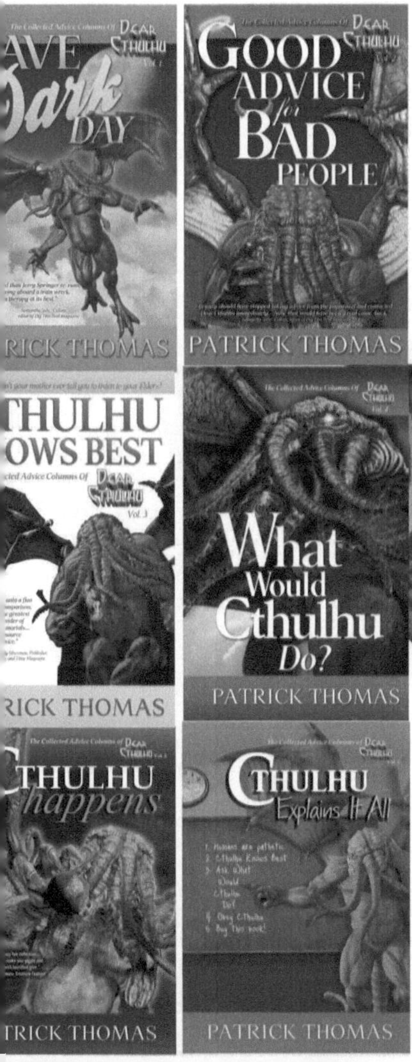

DEAR CTHULHU

THE ADVICE
COLUMN TO
***END* ALL**
ADVICE COLUMNS

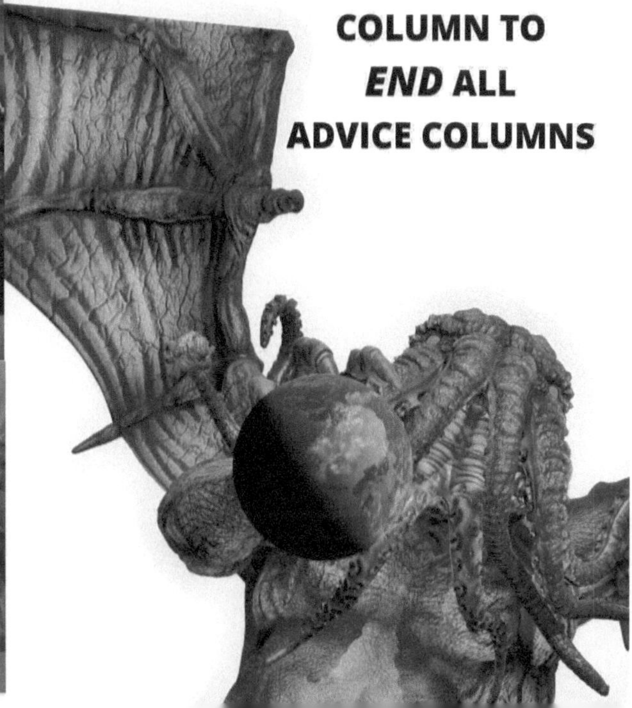